J

DISCARDED c op. 1

WEILERSTEIN, Sadie (Rose) 1895-

K'tonton in Israel. Illus. by Elizabeth
Safian. [N.Y.] National Women's League of
the United Synagogue of America [1964]
176p. illus.
Sequel to The adventures of K'tonton.

I. tc.

I4875-10 F

K'TONTON IN ISRAEL

K'TONTON

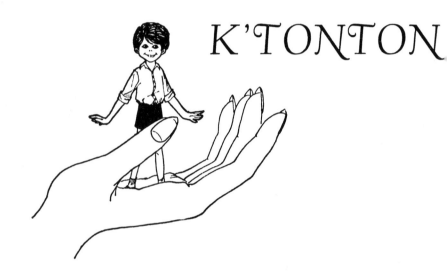

NATIONAL WOMEN'S LEAGUE

IN ISRAEL

by Sadie Rose Weilerstein

Illustrations by Elizabeth Safian

OF THE UNITED SYNAGOGUE OF AMERICA

Library of Congress Catalogue Card Number 64-24294

Copyrighted by

The National Women's League of the
United Synagogue of America

To

Ophra	Lauren
Noga	Daniel
Asaph	Faith
Ehud	Abby
Yonatan	Rachel
Dorit	Susan
Moshe	Lois
Yisrael	Margot
Meir	Barbara
Yehiel	Debra
Avram	Lisa
	Danny

in Israel

in America

and to

Baruch Reuben ז״ל

who delighted in them.

The National Women's League is proud to present this new publication, K'TONTON IN ISRAEL, a sequel to that perennial Jewish classic, THE ADVENTURES OF K'TONTON, which has delighted and captivated three generations of children.

We know that all children—and their mothers, too—will be fascinated with this mischievous and lovable Jewish Tom Thumb as they follow his adventures in Israel, starting his journey as a stowaway on an El Al plane.

For the past half century, the National Women's League of the United Synagogue of America has pioneered in the publication of books and recordings for Jewish women and children, enriching Jewish family living for its 200,000 members in all parts of the North American continent and serving far-flung areas of the world. We believe that K'TONTON IN ISRAEL is a worthy addition to our roster of books for the entertainment and education of the Jewish child, adding to his knowledge of Jewish folklore and tradition.

And so, settle down now, to many happy hours of delightful reading with our old-new friend, K'tonton.

Mrs. Albert Fried
National President

Contents

CONTENTS

Introducing K'tonton

THIS is K'tonton, a tiny Jewish boy. As you can see, he is no bigger than a thumb. Perhaps you have already met him in *The Adventures of K'tonton*, taking a ride on a chopping knife, spinning down the street on a runaway Ḥanukkah top, hiding in a plate of Purim goodies. K'tonton's curiosity, which was the biggest part of him, was always getting him into trouble and out of it.

Some of you have written to ask where K'tonton is now. He is in Israel and this book is about his adventures there, the happiest, most exciting of all his adventures.

You may remember that when K'tonton was a baby, his Mother used to set his cradle on the table where his father sat studying the Bible and Talmud. Back and forth his father swayed, reading out loud in a pleasant, singing tone. Back and forth K'tonton rocked in his cradle, listening. By the time he was able to run about and talk, he could recite Hebrew verses the way other children recite nursery rhymes. K'tonton was thankful for this when he came to Israel where the Bible stories happened and everybody speaks Hebrew.

Now we are ready for the adventures.

SHALOM!

(This is how one says "hello" and "goodbye" in Hebrew. It really means peace.)

K'tonton's official biographer,

S.R.W.

A Stowaway

No one in the airport knew that a tiny thumb-sized boy named K'tonton had arrived in Israel. The pilot of the El Al plane didn't know. The air hostess with the pleasant smile didn't know. The people who were saying *"Shalom! Sha-*

lom!" and hugging one another, and talking very fast—in Hebrew and English and Yiddish and German and French and Spanish—didn't know. The Israel customs officers didn't know. Not even Mrs. Levy-from-America knew, 'though she was the aunt of K'tonton's best friend, David.

K'tonton had come as a stowaway.

He was hiding in Mrs. Levy's overnight bag that very minute. Pit, pit, pat went his heart, so loud that he was sure somebody would hear it.

"Open the bag for inspection," said a voice.

The top of the bag was zipped open. K'tonton blinked his eyes as sunlight poured in. Up a pile of sweaters and handkerchiefs he climbed, and peeked out over the top. The bag was lying on a long table. Around it were other bags and suitcases. An officer near Mrs. Levy was reading from a paper.

"Is everything you've brought in on the list?" he asked.

K'tonton's heart beat faster. He had remembered that *he* wasn't on the list.

"I must get out before the inspector discovers me," he thought, climbing cautiously out of the bag. Down the side to the table he slid, down the table leg to the floor. Now he was scurrying in and out between people's feet. Now he had passed through the door and was standing in the dusty road. The dust reached to K'tonton's waist. It blew into his eyes, his mouth, his nose. It made him choke and sputter. A frown furrowed K'tonton's forehead—but only for a

4

minute. A joyful thought ironed it away: THIS WAS THE DUST OF ISRAEL.

"Abraham may have walked on this dust," K'tonton thought. "King David may have walked on this dust . . . Rabbi Akiba. . . ."

K'tonton planted his feet firmly in the dust of Israel and trudged on.

How did K'tonton happen to come to the Land of Israel? It had all begun the day before in his friend David's house. At the time he was sitting behind a candlestick high up on the mantelpiece. K'tonton had chosen the place so that he might see what was going on, without being seen. He had gotten so that he didn't like to be stared at and exclaimed over; and on this afternoon David's house was full of visitors, friends and relatives who had come to say goodbye to David's Aunt Minnie. Mrs. Levy —Aunt Minnie—was going to Israel for Passover. She wanted to celebrate the festival in Jerusalem as people used to do in Bible days.

5

"I wish *I* were going, Minnie," one of the cousins said. "Can't you take me along in your suitcase?" He pointed through the bedroom door to the suitcases piled on the floor.

"Crawl in," said Aunt Minnie, laughing.

Everybody laughed with her—*except K'tonton*. A tremendous, exciting thought had popped into K'tonton's head. He could get into the suitcase, even into the smallest one. That was the lucky part of being thumb-sized. He could slip into the suitcase and go up to the Land of Israel. On Passover he wouldn't say, "Next year in Jerusalem!" as he always did, he would *be* in Jerusalem.

K'tonton hurried across the mantel to the window and slid down the window drape to the floor. It took no more than a minute to reach the pile of luggage in the bedroom. The smallest bag, a cloth one with a zipper, was still open. Now to climb inside! K'tonton hurried to the far end of the room—to get a start—and made a running jump, right into the crease in the bag where the zipper began. He was taking hold of the leather tab, when he remembered something. *He hadn't asked his father and mother for permission.*

"But if I wait to ask permission, David's aunt will be gone," K'tonton thought.

He considered the matter. "Father says, 'If the chance to do a good deed, a *mitzvah,* comes to you, do it at once.

Don't delay.' Going up to Jerusalem is a very big *mitzvah*.
It says so in the Bible. Father wouldn't want me to put it
off. I'll leave a letter for him and explain."

He slid to the floor again. A piece of white wrapping
paper was lying nearby. K'tonton took a tiny pencil out of
his pocket. It was really a bit of lead broken off from a
pencil. In thin spidery letters he wrote:

> *Dear Father and Mother,*
>
> *I have found a way to go up to the Land of
> Israel so I am going. Please excuse me for not
> saying goodbye. There is no time, because the
> way I am going is in David's aunt's bag. It is a
> mitzvah to go up to Jerusalem for Pesah, so I
> knew you would not mind. As soon as I arrive I
> will send you a letter.*
>
> > *From me, your loving son,*
> > *K'tonton*
>
> *P.S. Do not worry that I will be hungry, Mother.
> My pockets are full of David's mother's honey
> cake.*

K'tonton folded the paper, wrote on the outside in the
biggest letters he could: "DEAR DAVID, PLEASE GIVE
THIS NOTE TO MY FATHER," and pinned it to a foot-
stool.

Then he leaped back into the fold of the bag and slipped
inside. Just in time!

"The taxi is here," someone called.

The zipper was pulled shut, the bag lifted.
K'tonton was on his way.

K'tonton could not have said how long he remained in the bag. He felt it swing to and fro, set down, lifted again. He heard voices:

"*Shalom, shalom!*"

"Have a good trip."

"To the International Airport!"

More noise! Bump! Honk, honk! A long, long ride, then voices again!

"That'll be six dollars!"

"Porter!"

"I'll carry the small bag with me."

The last voice was Mrs. Levy's. Again the bag was lifted, swung back and forth, set down. Now a roaring noise filled K'tonton's ears. A thread of light reached him as he snuggled at the bottom of the bag. He climbed toward it through hills of handkerchiefs, sweaters, tissues. The light was coming through a tiny opening where the zipper ended. Mrs. Levy had not zipped it quite shut. K'tonton stuck his little finger into the opening and pushed hard.

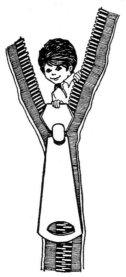

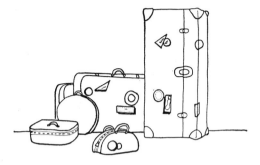

Now the hole was big enough for him to see through out of one eye.

An airplane loomed up before him, a giant bird with widespread wings. Hebrew letters ran across the body:

EL AL

K'tonton thought, "EL AL . . . that means *To the Sky.*" Just then the bag was lifted a third time, and K'tonton tumbled to the bottom. When he looked out again, he was inside the plane. The bag was on a seat near Mrs. Levy, its zipper wide open. K'tonton climbed out and made his way up a sweater to a window. Now he could see the giant wings spread out. The plane had mounted to the heavens. It was riding on the clouds. A verse from the Bible sang in K'tonton's heart.

I will make man little lower than the angels and will crown him with honor and glory.

K'tonton could feel the glory all around him. He was going to the Land of Israel.

Now you know how K'tonton came to be trudging along a dusty road outside the airport in Israel.

9

K'tonton Goes Up to Jerusalem

K'TONTON did not choose the car. It was the first one he came to outside the air-port. But he couldn't have found one better suited to him if he had tried. It was a very old car. The fender, bent and battered, almost reached the ground, so that K'tonton could reach it and hoist himself up. The dents in the metal gave him a foothold. The upholstery inside had torn places for his fingers to dig into. Up the back of the rear seat, K'tonton climbed. At the top, quite close to the window, was a perfect hole.

"I can hide in here and get a good view at the same time," K'tonton thought, as he fitted himself inside.

"Mind you, K'tonton didn't need to hide any more. Every Jew is welcome in the State of Israel. But being a stowaway had given him the habit of hiding.

The driver came up, threw a number of packages into

the trunk of the car, then got in. The engine coughed and chugged. The car was on its way. Only K'tonton and the driver were inside, and the driver didn't know that K'tonton was there. The rest of the tourists had chosen the shiny cars ahead.

Zoom, rattle, bang! The car sped down the road, then lurched around a corner. They were climbing into the hills, in and out along a corkscrew road. A signpost caught K'tonton's eye.

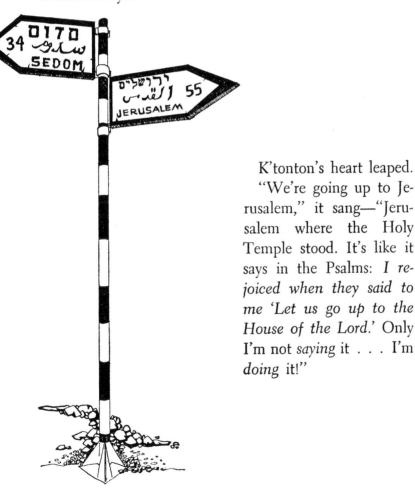

K'tonton's heart leaped. "We're going up to Jerusalem," it sang—"Jerusalem where the Holy Temple stood. It's like it says in the Psalms: *I rejoiced when they said to me 'Let us go up to the House of the Lord.'* Only I'm not *saying* it . . . I'm *doing* it!"

The song in K'tonton's heart rose up and up. He couldn't hold it back. It burst from his lips, thin, and sweet, and clear.

The driver heard it and turned. There on top of the rear seat, his feet fitted snugly in a hole in the upholstery, stood a tiny, thumb-sized boy.

"Shalom!" said the driver, looking interested but not surprised. He was used to seeing all kinds of Jews in Israel —blond Jews, black Jews, giant Jews from the Caucasus, brown lean Yemenite Jews with side curls, cave-dwelling Jews. This was a thumb-sized Jew.

"Shalom!" he said again. "Why do you sit there by yourself?" He grinned down at K'tonton. "The front seat upholstery also has good holes."

Without slowing down, he stretched out an arm to make a bridge for K'tonton to cross over.

From the top of the front seat, K'tonton looked up into the man's face. It was a pleasant face, browned by the sun and weather, with a nice big nose and blue eyes with wrinkles under them. "For the smiles to run down," K'tonton thought. The man's shirt was open at the neck. A beret was tipped back from his forehead.

"And where do you come from?" he asked, one eye on K'tonton, the other on the road, which at that moment was making a hairpin turn.

"I'm going up to Jerusalem," K'tonton said. He knew that this wasn't an answer to the question, but at the moment where he was going seemed more interesting than where he had come from.

The hills grew steeper and more barren. Stones and

boulders covered them. Suddenly K'tonton pointed excitedly. Lean brown men with pickaxes were splitting huge rocks apart.

"The stones! Are they iron?" K'tonton asked.

"Iron?"

K'tonton answered with a Bible verse: "*A land whose stones are iron and out of whose hills you may dig brass.*"

"I see you know your Bible," said the driver. "That makes you half an Israeli already. The stones you are talking about are down in the Negev near King Solomon's mines."

"Do you mean King Solomon who built the Holy Temple?" K'tonton's voice was full of awe.

"The very one! They're digging copper out of those old mines right now."

He was going to tell about the discovery of the ancient mines, but K'tonton's eyes were again on the hills. The dead, gray stones were gone. Grapevines rose in terraces. Pine trees covered the hill tops. Barns and neat red-roofed houses hid among green orchards.

"Trees!" K'tonton said in wonder. "Hills covered with trees! Maybe those are the ones the pennies from my blue-and-white box paid for. Maybe my tree that was planted when I was born is up there?"

He climbed out of the hole and leaned out of the window to get a better view.

A pull at his shirt brought him back.

"Easy there!" said the driver. "You're not trying to leave me, are you? I thought you wanted to go up to Jerusalem."

His blue eyes looked into K'tonton's dark eyes that were shining like stars.

"What did you say your name was?" he asked.

"I didn't say," K'tonton answered. "It's Isaac ben Baruch Reuben, for short K'tonton." Then in the same breath, "Are those Jewish National Fund trees? Are there any almond trees up there? Do you think there might be one my age, because . . ."

The man's eyes were laughing. "So your name is K'tonton. I thought it was Question Mark."

He pointed to a grove of olive trees ahead. Through the silvery tops rose the towers of Jerusalem. The car turned a corner.

"Where do you want to get off in Jerusalem, K'tonton?" he asked. "We're there."

They were on a noisy crowded street. People hurried in and out of stores, stood in long lines on the corners. Buses honked. . . .

Suddenly Jerusalem seemed to K'tonton very big and strange, very far from home.

"I'll get off at . . . at . . ." he hesitated.

"Because," the driver went on, "if you haven't any special place to go to, you could come home with me." He brought the car to a stop. "My wife would enjoy a guest for *Pesah*. You are so good at asking questions, you could ask the *Mah Nishtanah*." He meant the four questions the youngest child of the family asks on Passover Eve.

"Don't you have a son to ask?" K'tonton's eyes were filled with sympathy.

"Oh, I have a son all right, a fine, smart child," the driver assured him. "But he can't manage the *Mah Nishtanah* by himself. He's only a year and a half old."

"My father, too, has one son," K'tonton said gravely. "I don't know who will ask *him* the *Mah Nishtanah* this year."

Suddenly a tear slid down K'tonton's cheek and caught in a corner of his mouth. He sucked it in quickly.

"Sir. . . ." he began.

"My name is Shimshon," said the driver. "Now that we are friends, you must call me Shimshon."

"Shimshon," K'tonton spoke anxiously, "is it possible for a letter to be sent to America—very fast—so as to get there by *Pesah?*"

15

"Even before *Pesaḥ*," said Shimshon. "You shall write the letter and I will send it on the wings of the wind—that is to say on the wings of El Al." Again his eyes smiled. "I think you know something about those wings."

K'tonton nodded.

"Then everything is settled," Shimshon said. "You will go home with me and we shall mail the letter. On *Pesaḥ* you will help my Raphael ask the *Mah Nishtanah*. As you say in America, okay?"

"Okay," said K'tonton happily.

That night K'tonton wrote his letter.

Dear Father and Mother,
I arrived safely in Israel. Now I am in Jeru-salem, the Holy City. It is too wonderful to be-lieve. Shimshon brought me from the airport in

16

his taxi. He and Hannah want me to stay with them for Pesaḥ—also after Pesaḥ. Hannah is his wife.

I am teaching Raphael, the baby, the Mah Nishtanah. *Already he can say* mah. *If you would invite David's family for Pesaḥ, David could ask you the* Mah Nishtanah. *He doesn't know it by heart the way I do, but he can read it in the Haggadah.*

I miss you very much and hope you are not too upset. Maybe I shouldn't have gone without asking. But how could I lose the chance to go to Eretz Yisrael?

Please write me a letter soon.

Your loving son,
K'tonton

P.S. Hannah says you are not to worry about me. She says that God watches over the smallest of his creatures, and she, too, will keep an eye on me.

Passover had not yet arrived when an answer came.

To our dear and beloved son, K'tonton,

It was with joy and relief that we received your letter. We thank God that you have arrived safely in Israel. May Shimshon and his good wife be blessed for their kindness to you!

When David brought us your note, your mother and I did not know what to do. Should we call EL AL and ask them to send you back at once? Or should we let you stay since going up to the Land of Israel is a great mitzvah.

Your Mother said, "Why can't we go and bring him back ourselves? Then we, too, will see the Holy Land."

I answered her, "It is not so easy. We cannot go in somebody's suitcase like K'tonton. We must have plane or ship tickets."

So this is what we have decided. Since you are in good hands, you may stay until we save up for tickets to come and get you. We hope that this will be soon. I am writing to Shimshon to make arrangements. You must be careful to do whatever Shimshon and Hannah tell you, and to write us a letter every week. You know how your mother worries about you. She is sending your clothes and boots by air mail. I told her that you would not need boots. In Israel the rains come in winter. Now the dry season is beginning. But she is sending them anyway.

May God continue to watch over you!

With much love from your dear mother and from me, your father,

Baruch Reuben

A Passover Mix-Up

I DON'T know how I'd get my *Pesaḥ* cleaning done without K'tonton," Hannah said to Shimshon. "He's a bigger help to me than *you* are."

Shimshon pretended to be insulted.

"Name one thing K'tonton can do that I can't."

"Can *you* crawl into the coat pockets to look for crumbs?" Hannah asked. "And he's so good with Raphael."

"Say *mah nishtanah halailah hazeh*, Raphael," K'tonton urged.

"*Abba mah*," Raphael began. Then he stopped and grinned up at his father.

"That's as far as he'll go," K'tonton explained, apologetically. "I guess I'm not a very good teacher. He'll never be ready in time for the *seder*." The *seder*, the home celebration on Passover Eve, was only two days off.

"Raphael won't have to ask the *Mah Nishtanah this*

year," said Hannah. "We're going to the family *seder*. There'll be plenty of cousins to do the asking."

A look of dismay came into K'tonton's face.

"You'll come with us, of course, K'tonton," Hannah hurried to explain. "Did you think we'd leave you behind?"

But it wasn't the fear of being left behind that troubled K'tonton. It was the thought of all the new people he would have to meet.

"Could I go in Raphael's pocket?" he asked. Hannah had made Raphael a new shirt for Passover, a real boy's shirt with two pockets. "Raphael likes me to be near him. And . . . and . . ." K'tonton blurted it out. "If I went in his pocket, I'd be at the *seder* but nobody would know I was there."

"You can go any way you like," Hannah assured him. And that was how the mix-up came about.

The *seder* was at Shimshon's father's house. It was a low stone house with a garden in front and a tiled floor inside. When they came in, Shimson's mother was standing near the long table, arranging the pillows for his father to lean on. She dropped everything and gave Raphael a warm hug. K'tonton, hidden in Raphael's pocket, could feel the hug. It was just like his mother's. He almost climbed out to wish Raphael's grandmother good *Pesah*. Then he looked around at all the aunts and uncles and cousins, taking their places at the table, and he was glad he hadn't climbed out. There was a stern-looking uncle in a fur hat and a silk coat. There was an uncle in a frock coat and skull cap, and another like Shimshon in a white shirt and no tie. There were

20

girl cousins and boy cousins. The youngest one was practicing the *Mah Nishtanah* under his breath. The grandfather called him Meirke.

Then the service began and K'tonton forgot all about the company. It was exactly like his father's *seder*. K'tonton knew the words so well, he had to be careful not to say them out loud. First the *kiddush,* the blessing over the wine; then "Let all who are hungry come and eat"; then greens dipped in salt water. K'tonton managed to nibble a tiny bit of Raphael's.

Now the grandfather turned toward Raphael. There was a twinkle like Shimshon's in his eyes.

"Well, Raphael," he said, "are you ready to ask the *Mah Nishtanah?* You're the youngest son, you know."

Everybody smiled. The next minute the smiles turned to amazement. From Raphael's place a voice was rising, thin but sweet and clear: *"Mah Nishtanah halailah hazeh mikol halaylot?"* (Why is this night different from all other nights?) Raphael the *baby,* was asking the *Mah Nishtanah.* Who had ever heard of such a wonder?

Only Hannah and Shimshon knew that the voice was K'tonton's, not Raphael's. Mind you, K'tonton had not meant to speak. It was just that he was so used to asking the four questions. When the proper moment came, he had spoken up without thinking. Now he crouched down in Raphael's pocket, dismayed at the thing that he had done. He wished that he could hide forever. He wished that he were *smaller* than a *k'tonton,* that he could shrink into a pin-point.

21

The family was waiting breathlessly for Raphael to go on. K'tonton could see them through one eye. Clearest of all, he could see Meirke. A tear was running down Meirke's cheek. *He* had expected to ask the *Mah Nishtanah*. He had practiced it and practiced it.

"Now he can't ask on account of me," K'tonton thought in distress. "And it's his right to ask. Except for Raphael, he's the youngest at the table."

K'tonton's head was whirling. He looked pleadingly toward Shimshon. Shimshon's lips formed the words, "Shall I tell?"

K'tonton nodded yes.

Shimshon threw him a quick smile, then turned toward his father.

"Father, family," he said, "I am flattered that you think our Raphael is already a *Ḥaham,* but the truth is that he is still a *She'ayno-yoday'a-lishol.*"

You remember that the *Ḥaham* was the wise son of the *Haggadah,* and the *She'ayno-yoday'a-lishol,* the son who wasn't able to ask.

Shimshon continued, "We have a guest at our *seder.* It was he who began to ask the questions—by mistake." He lifted K'tonton out of Raphael's pocket and set him on the table. "It gives me pleasure to present K'tonton ben Baruch Reuben, lately arrived in Israel."

A gasp ran round the table. A thumb-sized guest! This was even more amazing than having a baby ask the four questions. Every eye in the room was on K'tonton.

But K'tonton was too relieved to mind. Meirke had

arisen and was asking the *Mah Nishtanah*. Straight through the four questions he went, his voice filled with happiness. But not even Meirke was as happy as K'tonton. The wrong he hadn't meant to do, had been righted.

From K'tonton's letter to his Father and Mother:

> . . . *So everything is now* beseder. *That is how you say "okay" in Israel. Meirke and I are friends. I am going to give him all my stamps from America. You can save the Israel stamps for David.*
>
> *Over and over I keep saying: "This year I am in Jerusalem." Only one thing is missing. You are missing.*
>
> > *With much love from me, your son,*
> > *K'tonton*
>
> *P.S. Are you wondering what one says in Israel for "Next year in Jerusalem?" One says, "Next year in Jerusalem rebuilt!" But I also said, "Next year Father and Mother in Jerusalem!"*
>
> *P.S.2 Thank you, thank you for letting me stay! You will see how careful I will be.*

K'tonton Meets the President of Israel

I︎T happened during the week of Passover. Shimshon had a package to deliver and took K'tonton with him. Even the car looked *Pesaḥdig*.
It had a new coat of paint—Shimshon's work—and new slip-
covers to hide the holes in the seats—Hannah's work.

"That's the house of the *Nasi*, the President," Shimshon
said, pointing to a white stone house beyond a park path.

"Yehudah Hanasi's house?" K'tonton asked wonder-
ingly.

Yehudah Hanasi was a famous rabbi who lived more
than a thousand years ago. But K'tonton's head was so full
of stories from the Bible and the Talmud that sometimes
what happened a thousand years ago, seemed as real to him
as what was happening that day.

"Not that *Nasi*," Shimshon explained patiently. "The
President of the *State of Israel*. Have you forgotten that we

again have a *Nasi,* a President? Today is his Passover reception."

"What's a reception?" K'tonton asked.

"A kind of party. You go in and shake hands with the President and his wife."

"Could *I* go in?" K'tonton asked.

"You could if you wanted to. Everybody in the land is invited."

Shimshon stopped the car. "Wait here, K'tonton," he said, as he picked up a package. "I'll be right back." And Shimshon disappeared in a doorway.

K'tonton sat thinking. "The President of the State of Israel is in that house. Shimshon said I could go in . . . if I wanted to. I *want* to!"

He slid down the seat and out through the open door. Across the walk, strewn with seeds from the pepper trees, into the park K'tonton ran. K'tonton went past them all to a lamppost with a vine twining around it. Up the vine he climbed and looked back.

Everybody had come to meet the President. K'tonton saw old people and young people; city people and country people; hikers in shorts, knapsacks hanging from their shoulders; men like Shimshon's uncle, in fur hats and silken coats. A black-eyed baby, riding on its mother's back, laughed up at him.

K'tonton was wondering how the baby managed to hold on with just his legs twined round her waist, when a group of tourists came down the path. A guide was leading them. Past all the waiting people they went, straight to the head of the line.

An angry voice rose from the back. "*Protectsia!* Why do *they* have special pull? Let them wait their turn like everyone else!"

K'tonton felt his cheeks burn with shame. He had remembered that he too had gone past the crowd to the head of the line.

"I must go back . . . at once," K'tonton decided. "That soldier was the last in line when I came in. I remember the sweater tied round his neck by the sleeves. That's where I belong."

He slipped from the lamppost to the nearest head. It was a hatless head with a thatch of blonde hair. Back and back, from one head to the next, K'tonton leaped. People were pressed so closely together, it wasn't hard. Now K'tonton landed on a bright turban, now on a woman's head shawl, now on a little round cap, a *kipah*, no bigger than a silver dollar. The *kipah* was pinned to a boy's curly head with a bobby pin.

K'tonton knew it wasn't polite to walk on people's heads. But the crowd had grown so big, he would have been crushed underfoot on the ground. "It's a case of *piku'ah nefesh*, the saving of a life," K'tonton told himself. "If anyone notices me, I'll explain." But nobody *did* notice him. The people were too busy pushing and jostling. The soldier, K'tonton was trying to reach, had turned around to talk to someone behind him. Between him and K'tonton stood a bald-headed man. K'tonton tried to land on the bald head as lightly as possible, but he wasn't light enough. Up went the man's hand to see what had bounced down on him. K'tonton barely escaped his fingers. He slid down the back of the man's head into the sweater on the soldier's back. Patiently, K'tonton settled down in the folds of the sweater to wait his turn.

The door to the President's house opened and the crowd lunged forward. K'tonton, high up in the soldier's back, passed through. At once the noise and jostling stopped. The line moved slowly, respectfully. They entered a beautiful, quiet room. K'tonton's eyes turned eagerly toward the President and his wife. The President's hand went out to each one who passed, but his eyes did not smile. A furrow creased his forehead. It was his wife who smiled and talked to the people.

"The President is tired," K'tonton thought. "No wonder! He has the whole country to think about. He has all the people returning from the four corners of the earth to think about."

Some of the *olim*, the immigrants, were right there in

the room. They leaned against the walls, squatting on the soles of their feet. Among them was the mother of the black-eyed baby. A boy, also with black eyes, sat beside them quite close to the President. K'tonton saw him take a cloth bag from his mother's lap, open it wide and stick in his hand.

At that moment the line moved on. K'tonton's turn had come at last. He slid to the floor, threw back his head and looked up into the face of the PRESIDENT OF THE STATE OF ISRAEL. Something began rising inside K'tonton, up and up from the pit of his stomach to his throat. It was a song. There was wonder in it. There were pride and gladness and thanksgiving—

> *David Melekh Yisrael*
> *Ḥai, ḥai, vekayam!*
> David, King of Israel, lives,
> Lives on forever.

The song leaped into the air and K'tonton leaped after it, dancing joyously.

The President heard it and looked down. A look of wonder came into his eyes. He smiled. Then he turned to his wife to see whether she, too, had seen.

When he looked again, K'tonton was no longer there.

"I must be more tired than I thought," the President said, laughing. "I actually imagined a little fellow was dancing in front of me—no bigger than this." He stuck out a thumb to show her.

When he turned to shake hands with the next person in line, his eyes were still smiling.

The President was not the only one who had seen K'tonton dancing. A buzz ran through the house. From person to person it passed, from one room to the next. A tiny thumb-sized fellow had danced before the President.

"It couldn't be," laughed the blue-eyed girl who was serving punch and Passover cookies to the visitors—Israelis from the cities and settlements, tourists, immigrants from Yemen and Persia and Iraq and Roumania. "Whoever heard of a thumb-sized person?"

"I *saw* him," said a little Moroccan boy, reaching for his sixth cookie. He was the boy K'tonton had seen sticking his hand into his mother's bag.

"How do you know it couldn't be?" asked a jolly policeman. "Stranger things have happened in Israel."

"Ridiculous!" This time a man with thick eyeglasses was speaking. "If a thumb-sized person danced before the President, where is he now?"

You would never guess where K'tonton was. He was inside the cloth lunch bag the mother of the black-eyed boy was carrying. Mind you, nobody knew that he was in the bag. K'tonton, himself, didn't know. He lay at the bottom in a jumble of broken *matzot*, sunflower seeds, cucumbers, too dazed to realize what was going on.

To explain how K'tonton had gotten there, we must go back to the moment when he was dancing before the President. You remember that the little boy—his name was

29

Shalom—had just opened his mother's bag to get at the sunflower seeds inside. The sight of a thumb-sized boy dancing before the President so astonished him that the bag slid from his hands to the floor. Its opening was practically underneath K'tonton. One minute K'tonton was leaping joyfully in the air. The next minute he had come down, not on the floor, but in a fold in the open sack. Before he could get out, the bag was snatched up. Down to the bottom K'tonton tumbled, hitting his head against a hard cucumber. That's why he was still lying in a daze.

Though Shalom had seen K'tonton going up, he hadn't seen him coming down. At that moment he was getting a scolding from his mother.

"Have you a hole in your belly that you must always be eating?" his mother scolded. "You'll get sunflower seeds all over the President's floor."

She picked the bag up by its strings and jerked it shut.

By the time K'tonton came out of his daze, the black-eyed boy and his family had left the President's house. The bag was swinging back and forth. K'tonton could tell by the food scraps around him that he was in somebody's lunch bag. But he didn't know whose.

"I must get out. I must find a way to climb to the top," he thought. But when he tried to stand on his feet, he swayed dizzily.

The swinging stopped at last. A brown hand came down into the bag. It was a small child's hand, but it didn't seem small to K'tonton. The hand groped for a fistful of sunflower seeds. Instead it closed over K'tonton. Up, up K'tonton went, blinking as light poured into the sack.

A boy was looking down at him, a little boy with black eyes and tousled hair. His mouth, opened in a smile, showed shining white teeth.

"You're the one who danced for the President," said the boy in a pleased voice. "You're *real!*"

"Of course I'm real." K'tonton spoke with irritation. He had been having a trying time. "I'm K'tonton ben Baruch Reuben, come up to the Land of Israel. Why did you think I wasn't real?"

"The lady said so."

"What lady?"

"The lady in the President's house who gave us cookies." The boy laughed. "The President liked to see you dance. You made him smile. Will you dance for me? Will you sing the David song?"

"I haven't time," said K'tonton. "I must get right back to Shimshon."

"Why?"

"Because I live with him. He'll be worried about me."

"Why?"

K'tonton thought it was his turn for questions. "You haven't told me your name," he said.

"I'm Shalom! That's my mother and those are my brothers and sister." He waved toward the other side of the room. A woman with a shawl wound around her head was stirring a pot. "This is our cousin's house. We've come for *Pesah.* Tomorrow we're going up Mount Zion. If you stay, you can go with us."

"Mount Zion!" K'tonton's heart leaped. If he stayed, he could go up to Mount Zion. He'd be a pilgrim, an *oleh regel*, like in the Bible days.

K'tonton knew that he should be hurrying back to Hannah and Shimshon. But how could he *not* go up to Mount Zion?

"Will you stay? Will you?" Shalom begged.

K'tonton nodded his head.

"*Todah rabbah!* . . . Thank you very much for asking me," he added.

Shalom was already at the other end of the room.

"Mother, Mother! The size-of-a-thumb-one who danced for the President, he's. . . ."

"Are you still talking about that one?" scolded his mother. "All day you eat and when it comes time to eat, you talk. Not another word out of you! Wash your hands and sit down to your supper."

She set the pot on the table and began ladling out the food. Steam arose, teasing Shalom's nose with the good smell of vegetables and lamb. He sat down with the others and dipped into his plate, using a chunk of *matzah* for a spoon. But he didn't forget K'tonton. When his stomach was full, he broke off a tiny piece of *matzah*, and piled it with bits of the spicy stew. Then he brought it to K'tonton, hidden behind the bag, followed by an almond shell of water.

"Now sing the David song," Shalom begged, when K'tonton's stomach was also full. And K'tonton sang, softly so that no one but Shalom might hear.

David Melekh Yisrael
Ḥai, ḥai, vekayam

"Again," said Shalom.

K'tonton sang it a second time, a third.

His eyes were blinking, his head nodding. He curled up on the soft bag, murmured his nighttime prayer and slept.

New Friends Lost—
Old Friends Found

*E*ARLY the next morning Shalom and his family stood in the crowd at the foot of Mount Zion. K'tonton was with them, tucked into Shalom's waistband. The shirt tail, which had a way of creeping out, made a little tent for him to hide under. K'tonton threw back his head and looked up. High up at the top was King David's Tomb.

"I ought to be going up on foot," K'tonton thought. A pilgrim is supposed to go on foot. But how can I? There must be fifty steps, a hundred steps, more than a hundred. And each one is three times as high as I am. That's the trouble with being a k'tonton!"

An idea came to him. He would go up on Shalom's foot.

"Hist, Shalom!" K'tonton called up, "Would you mind if I slide down your foot?"

"Why?" asked Shalom.

"So I can be a pilgrim, a foot traveler."

"You won't see anything down there," said Shalom. But he bent over obligingly, lifted K'tonton from his waistband and tucked him into his shoe.

So K'tonton went up Mount Zion on Shalom's foot. But he didn't come down with Shalom. By the time Shalom's mother had lit a candle at King David's Tomb, and said a prayer, K'tonton was off on a new adventure.

The new adventure began two flights up on the roof of the building over David's Tomb. K'tonton had hitched a ride up the stairs on a tourist's walking stick. He had a special reason for going up. Shimshon had once told him that from the roof one could get a view into the Old City. That was the part of Jerusalem where the Holy Temple had once stood.

K'tonton was standing on the parapet, solemnly looking down on the ancient wall, wondering which part was the *Kotel Hama'aravi*, the wall of the Holy Temple, when a voice startled him.

"Grandpa Ya'akov, look! There's K'tonton."

K'tonton turned quickly. A boy was pointing to him.

"Do you know me?" K'tonton asked in surprise.

"Of course I know you," said the boy. "You're in my book. You look just like your pictures. Doesn't he, Grandpa?" he asked, turning to the gray-haired man beside him.

"I didn't know my book had come to Israel, too," said K'tonton, looking even more surprised.

"It's in my grandma's house. I've read all your adventures. You had some pretty exciting ones, didn't you? And you were always getting lost. You're not lost now, are you?"

"No," said K'tonton. "I'm in the Land of Israel."

"With your father and mother, K'tonton?" This time it was the grandfather who spoke.

"No," said K'tonton. "They're in America. I . . . I live with Shimshon and Hannah and Raphael. I'd better go back to them now. They might be worrying about me."

K'tonton's voice sounded as if he himself were a little worried. He had remembered that he didn't know how to get back.

"First let us introduce ourselves," said the grandfather. "This is Yonatan and I am Grandpa Ya'akov. Now then, can you tell me where Shimshon lives?"

"In Sha'aray . . . Sha'aray. . . ." K'tonton hesitated.

"Sha'aray Hesed?"

K'tonton nodded, relieved.

"That's next to Rehavia where we live," said the grandfather. "Do you know the name of the street in Sha'aray Hesed?"

K'tonton didn't remember. He knew only that the street had the name of a famous person. But almost all the streets in Jerusalem are named after famous people, so that wasn't much help.

"Suppose you come home with me and Yonatan," said the grandfather. "Then we'll see if we can't find Shimshon. You'll be nearer to him at our house than you are here."

"Please come, K'tonton, please! You can ride in Grandpa Ya'akov's hatband."

"That's his favorite place," he explained to his grandfather.

Grandpa Ya'akov bent down. He wasn't a tall man, but he was a very pleasant one.

K'tonton climbed into his hatband, and that's where he was when Yonatan's grandmother first saw him.

"We've brought you a guest from America," said Grandpa, when she opened the apartment door for them. He was holding his hat behind his back. "Who is it? I'll give you three guesses."

Yonatan's grandmother couldn't have guessed if they had given her a hundred guesses. In the end Grandpa Ya'akov had to hold up his hat for her to see, and then she hardly believed her eyes.

"K'tonton!" she cried, "Whoever thought I'd see you in Israel! Though why shouldn't I have thought it?" she added.

Then she asked him about his mother and his father and his Aunt Gittel and Uncle Israel. And she made him eat a delicious dinner—a wee ball of *gefilte* fish, a whole thimbleful of knadel soup, and the tip-of-a-spoonful of *tsimmes*.

"You cook just like my mother," K'tonton told her.

Afterward, he and Yonatan sat on the floor looking at the pictures in his book.

"That's where you took a ride on the chopping knife," Yonatan said. "Did I laugh when you fell into the chopped fish!"

"I don't see what's so funny about it," said K'tonton. "Those awful blades going chop, chop, chop! I was sure it was the end of me."

"But it wasn't. That was just the beginning of your adventures. Do you remember in the *sukkah*, when you asked the eggshell bird to carry you to the Land of Israel? Well, now you're here."

K'tonton nodded happily. "When did *you* come to Israel, Yonatan?" he asked.

"I didn't come, I'm a *sabra*. I was born here." Yonatan answered proudly.

"Was your mother born here?"

"No. She was born in Holland. Grandpa Ya'akov came here from America . . . years and years ago with Henrietta Szold. He's a dentist."

K'tonton jumped to his feet.

"That's it! That's it!" he cried excitedly.

"That's what?" Yonatan asked, puzzled.

"The name of the street where Shimshon lives, Reḥov Henrietta Szold. I told you it had the name of an important person. Henrietta Szold *was* an important person, wasn't she?"

"She sure was," said Yonatan. "The Hospital and Clinic

and the Nurses' school were all her idea. She's a *very* important person."

So K'tonton got back to Shimshon at last. Yonatan's grandfather took him over to Henrietta Szold Street and K'tonton pointed out the house.

Shimshon himself opened the door.

"Come quick, Hannah. It's K'tonton," he cried.

Raphael heard him and squealed with delight. Hannah came running.

"I told you he'd be back," said Shimshon. "Women! Always worrying!"

Hannah didn't answer. She had taken K'tonton in her hand and was pressing him to her cheek the way his mother did.

From K'tonton's letter to his Father and Mother:

> . . . *Father, Mother, there is once more a* Nasi, *a President, in the Land of Israel. I myself saw him. A small accident followed but* gam zu leto-vah, *this, too, was for the best, because afterward I went up Mount Zion. I went on Shalom's foot, not mine, on account of the steepness of the stairs. Shalom is my new friend. He is one of the* olim. *Also I have another friend, Yonatan. He knew me from my book.*
>
> *Yonatan is a* sabra. *Shimshon says if you are born in Israel people call you a* sabra, *because the* sabra *is a kind of cactus which is prickly*

outside but sweet inside. But Yonatan is nice on both sides.

If David reads my letter, please tell him not to mind about my new friends. He is still my best friend.

> *From me, your loving son,*
> *K'tonton*

Wisdom from a Donkey

K'TONTON walked along a lane between high stone walls. The smile, which had been growing wider and wider since the day he arrived in Israel, had suddenly disappeared. A frown puckered his forehead. At whom was he frowning? At *himself.*

"Here I am," he thought, "come at last to the Land of Israel. All around me is work waiting to be done, stones to gather, rocks to crush, swamps to drain, deserts to water, forests to plant, houses to build. I should have been a giant. And what am I? A k'tonton!"

He squinted his eyes upward, then glanced down.

"Four inches from head to toe," he said in disgust. "What can you do with four inches?"

At that moment K'tonton noticed the donkey. It was hitched to an oil cart near a gate in the stone wall. While its master was in the houses delivering the oil, the donkey cropped the weeds that grew beside the road.

It was the weeds that caught K'tonton's eye. They were thistles, tall prickly thistles. How could the donkey eat thistles without getting the prickles in its tongue? Curiosity made K'tonton forget his worries. If there was one thing in K'tonton that wasn't tiny, it was his curiosity. He went closer to the donkey to get a better look, then remembered that the donkey might gobble him up along with the thistles. Not deliberately! Donkeys are vegetarians. But it might gobble him up by accident.

"If it did, I'd get a good inside view of its tongue," K'tonton thought, grinning. "But I guess I'd better get an outside view—from above."

A bougainvillea vine, gay with blossoms, covered the wall. K'tonton took hold of a branch. Up and up he climbed, then sprang lightly to the donkey's back. Running the length of its back was easy. Climbing downhill along its bent neck was harder, but K'tonton made it. By kneeling between its long ears and leaning forward, he could look straight down the donkey's nose to its mouth. K'tonton watched intently as the tongue came out. *It was hard and leathery.*

"So that's why you can eat thistles! You have a leather tongue." K'tonton laughed aloud, pleased with himself for having solved the puzzle.

Maybe it was the laughter that startled the donkey. Maybe K'tonton had stepped on a ticklish place between its ears. Suddenly it lifted its head and opened its jaws wide. Out came a squeaking hee, followed by a tremendous HAW—a giant haw, an earth-shaking—at least a K'tonton-

shaking—HAW. K'tonton tumbled down among the this-tles.

"And *my* skin isn't leathery," he thought ruefully, as the thistles pricked and scratched his cheeks.

A second hee-HAW followed. This one had a reproach-ful sound. The donkey was looking directly at K'tonton. It seemed to be talking to him.

"Maybe the donkey *is* talking to me," K'tonton thought, "the way the ass talked to Balaam in the Bible. The Bible says it spoke, but it doesn't say what language it spoke. Maybe it was donkey language. Maybe this donkey has a message for *me*."

A third time the donkey opened its mouth wide and brayed. Its tongue showed clearly, dark and hard and leath-ery.

This time K'tonton understood. The donkey was saying, "You ought to be ashamed of yourself, K'tonton, com-plaining about your size. God gave *me* a leathery tongue. Do I complain? No! I use it to clear the land of thistles. *If you have no BIGNESS to help with, help with your little-ness!*"

"Thank you, donkey. That's just what I'll do," K'tonton said humbly.

He crawled out of the clump of thistles, too excited to feel the scratches. "I'll search," he said, "until I find a way."

The very next day K'tonton discovered the Clinic. Yedid-ya, Shimshon's neighbor who had come from Yemen, worked there as a porter. But it wasn't with Yedidya that

K'tonton set out that morning. It was with Shirah, his wife. Shirah had stopped in to see Hannah on her way to the girls' school where she worked. Shirah embroidered beautiful Yemenite patterns for the girls at the school to copy.

She was in the kitchen talking to Hannah, and the embroideries were rolled up on the table when K'tonton began playing peek-a-boo with Raphael. He didn't hide his face behind his fingers as he usually did. This time he hid the whole of himself inside the roll of embroideries.

Out K'tonton ran.

"I see you!" he called.

Raphael's face broke into a big smile.

In K'tonton ran. The smile vanished. In! Out! In! Out!

K'tonton was *in* when Shirah returned from the kitchen and picked up her roll of embroideries. Now, K'tonton could have called to Shirah that he was inside the roll. But he knew that she was on her way to work, and K'tonton could not resist going to new places. He held on to the cloth, keeping very still.

After a long, long time and much bumping and many kinds of noises—bus noises, people noises, doors-opening-and-shutting noises—he felt the roll laid down. Steps tapped. Was Shirah leaving him? K'tonton peeked out of the roll. What he saw made his mouth fall open in astonishment. Before him was a VILLAGE OF K'TONTONS. A tiny scribe bent over a scroll. People squatted on the ground. A woman in a head shawl and a gaily striped dress carried a basket on her head. Beyond them, a wee horse hitched to a farm wagon, stood waiting. Tiny sheep grazed.

45

A shepherd held a flute to his lips. *Not a person among them was half the size of K'tonton.*

For the first time in his life K'tonton could look *down* on people instead of looking *up* at them. It was a wonderful feeling.

"*Shalom,*" he said, trying to talk in a deep-down voice.

Nobody answered. Not only did nobody answer; nobody stirred.

K'tonton drew nearer. *These weren't people!* They were tiny colored figures carved out of wood. The colors, painted on so skillfully, had made them look real.

K'tonton knew that he wasn't a giant, after all. He was just a k'tonton standing on a table. But he could *pretend* to be a giant. He stood up tall, legs apart, arms clasped over his chest, and spoke.

"Do not be afraid of me, my good people. It is true, you are no more than grasshoppers beside me, but I am no son of Goliath. I . . ." K'tonton never finished the sentence. The door had opened, and a young girl entered the room followed by a group of tourists, all chattering in English.

"Look at those tiny figures," one of the women cried, hurrying over to the table. "Are they for sale?"

"Everything on the table is for sale," the young girl explained.

"I'll take that one. He looks almost real."

K'tonton saw with horror that the woman was pointing at *him*. She turned to the girl to ask the price. K'tonton looked around wildly for a place to hide. Someone had laid an open camera case on the table. K'tonton slipped inside and crouched down under the cover—just in time.

"Did you say you wanted this one?" The young girl picked up the shepherd with the flute.

"No! No!" the woman cried. "The bigger one—with the shorts." Her eyes ran across the little figures. "It was here, just a second ago."

At that moment, someone looked in through the door and called that their car was waiting. They'd have to leave if they wanted to visit the Clinic.

The woman who had set down her camera picked it up and hung it from her shoulder. K'tonton, hidden underneath the half-open cover, smiled. He had seen the school where Shirah worked. Now he was on his way to the Hospital Clinic where Yedidya worked.

The long corridor of the Clinic was full of children with their mothers and fathers, waiting their turn to see the doctors. They sat on wooden benches; they stood in a long line, each grownup with a slip of paper in his hand. Nurses passed in and out.

The grownups waited patiently, thinking anxious thoughts. The children wiggled and pulled at their mothers' skirts. They didn't like waiting. A tousle-headed boy climbed over a bench and got a spanking from his father. He opened his mouth and bawled. "Ow—w—w—ou—!" Two little sisters in pink starched dresses bawled in sympathy. A baby, frightened by the noise, began crying. A little Arab girl, bangles on her forehead, looked as if *she* were going to cry. So did a sad-eyed boy with side curls peeking out beneath a bandage on his head. *All* the children began crying.

A pretty nurse in a ponytail hurried in, but she couldn't stop them. The fathers and mothers couldn't stop them.

Suddenly, the children stopped by themselves. The tousle-headed boy, who had started the trouble, began laughing instead of crying. The sad-eyed boy with the bandaged head smiled. The Arab girl put her hand to her mouth—the good hand that wasn't in a sling—and stared, her eyes under the bangles full of wonder. The sisters in the pink starched dresses laughed out loud. All the children were laughing.

The parents sighed with relief. The nurse with the ponytail laughed. "It's as catching as the measles," she said to a doctor who had opened his door to see what the commotion was about. "One child bawls, they all begin bawling. A child laughs . . . and look at them! You'd think they were watching a circus."

The grownups didn't know it, but the children *were* watching a circus, or rather a circus clown. He was a tiny clown, no more than four inches tall, and he didn't wear a clown's suit. But he did handsprings, and somersaults and flip-flops like a clown. He was so funny, the children couldn't help laughing. They didn't mind waiting their turn any more. They didn't even want their turn to come.

The clown, of course, was K'tonton. He had arrived at the Clinic and managed to get out of the camera case just as the crying began. He almost joined in the crying. Then he remembered how long ago on a Purim day, he had made a sad, sick-in-bed little boy laugh. He remembered that only the week before he had made the President of the State of Israel laugh. The first thing he knew, he was turn-

ing cartwheels and somersaults to make the children laugh.

All the rest of the day K'tonton kept watch on the children from a hiding-place under a bench. At the first sight of a frown, he ran out and performed.

Once a little boy said right out loud, "Look at the tiny tumbler doing tricks! Look at him, Father." But his father didn't hear. He was too busy trying to see how many people were ahead of them.

"What imaginations children have!" a nurse said to another nurse, without looking down.

K'tonton was greatly relieved. He didn't want any grownup to see him because he didn't have a slip of paper. He wasn't sure you could stay in the Clinic if you didn't have a slip of paper like the rest of the people—unless you were a doctor or a nurse or worked there like Yedidya.

The thought of Yedidya brought Hannah and Raphael to mind. Had Hannah worried when he disappeared so suddenly? Did Raphael miss him? How could he get back to them?

Now it was K'tonton who was thinking anxious thoughts. He didn't notice when the last person left the Clinic. He didn't notice how quiet the room had become. He didn't look up until a broom brushed against his cheek. Yedidya was pushing the broom.

"Yedidya," K'tonton called joyfully. "It's me! K'tonton! Will you take me home? Will you bring me back tomorrow?"

Yedidya stooped.

"The tiny one!" he exclaimed. "What are you doing here?"

"Helping," K'tonton answered, "with my littleness."

From K'tonton's letter to his Father and Mother:

> . . . *So now I am helping with my littleness the way the donkey said. Every morning Yedidya takes me to the Clinic, but tomorrow we will not go because it will be a holiday, Yom Ha'-atsma'ut, Israel's Independence Day. Shimshon says there will be a big parade. First we will go to the synagogue. Then Yonatan's grandfather*

will take us to see the parade. Shimshon will be in it because he is a veteran.

Your loving son,
K'tonton

P.S. Maybe you do not know about Yom Ha'-atsma'ut because it is a new holiday, so I will tell you about it. The Nations of the World—United Nations—said, "We will divide Palestine. Part will be for the Arabs and part for the Jews. They will live in peace, and bring water to the land and plant and build. And Jerusalem will be for everybody."

But the Arab nations did not want a State of Israel. Five armies came with guns, and tanks, and grenades, and airplanes with bombs. They attacked Jerusalem and all the cities and villages of Israel. But with God's help the few can win against the many. The Jews fought hard for their land, and Israel and Jerusalem were saved . . . except the old part of Jerusalem behind the walls. They could not save the old part. So now there is a border with barbed wire, and we cannot visit the Holy Places.

I have more to tell you, but Shimshon says, "Why is the tail of your letter longer than the letter? We will miss the mailman." So I will close.

P.S. 2 On this side of the border there are also Arabs, but these live in peace with us. Israel is their State also.

K'tonton Is Mistaken for a Puppet

*I*T happened on *Yom Ha'atsma'ut*, Israel's Independence Day. The National Fund Building was crowded with visitors who had come over after the parade. K'tonton, tucked into Grandpa Ya'akov's hatband, could hear the guide talking about a book he called the *Sefer Bar Mitzvah*.

"In the *Sefer Bar Mitzvah*," the guide was saying, "you will find names and pictures of boys and girls from all over the world."

K'tonton craned his neck to get a glimpse of the book. But Grandpa Ya'akov was not a very tall man. All K'tonton could see was people's heads. He climbed out of the hatband, grabbed hold of a framed picture on the wall, and made his way to the top. Now he had a much better view. A group of boys and girls from a youth village were bending over the open book, trying to read the inscriptions.

"Here's somebody from England."

"This one's from Mexico City."

"Look! Here's a girl who lives in Brook-lyn-New-York. That's in the United States."

The book was closed. The leader of the group called out, "Keep close together as we leave the building. Our next stop will be Ramat Raḥel."

Ramat Raḥel! This was the *kibbutz*, the settlement, that had fought off two armies in the War of Liberation and saved Jerusalem. Shimshon said you could still see the bullet holes in the walls. K'tonton forgot that he had promised Hannah to stay close to Grandpa Ya'akov. All he could think of was how much he wanted to see Ramat Raḥel. The boys and girls were going there. He would ask to go along.

"If you please, will you give me a lift to Ramat Raḥel?"

Ari, the red-headed boy with the freckles, heard the small voice, and looked up. Perched on a frame that hung on the wall was a tiny boy, the size of a rather long thumb.

Ari, of course, didn't know about K'tonton. He didn't know there was such a thing as a thumb-sized person in the world.

"This is somebody's idea of a joke," he thought. "Probably one of Zev's puppets."

Zev was the tall, lanky boy behind him. Making puppets was Zev's hobby. He was the entertainer-in-chief of the village, puppeteer, ventriloquist, magician.

"I'll keep a straight face and pretend I think this is real," Ari decided.

He looked up at the tiny figure. "You're welcome to a lift," he said politely.

"*Todah rabbah*. Thank you very much," said the little fellow, and he hopped on the canteen that hung from Ari's shoulder.

"Now how did Zev manage that?" Ari wondered. "I don't see a sign of a string or a spring."

The leader was signaling them to start. Through the halls, down the stairs to the open court, went the boys and girls.

"Take a look at my canteen, Miriam," Ari said to the girl beside him, the one with the long thick braids. "One of Zev's masterpieces!"

"Oh, the darling puppet!" cried Miriam. "Let me take it."

"No," said Ari. "I want to try something!"

He stood still, letting Zev go ahead. Then he glanced down. The little fellow was still on the canteen.

"Zev must manipulate the thing by remote control. It's the only way I can figure out," said Ari. "That Zev is a genius."

Luckily, K'tonton was too busy with his thoughts to notice what was being said about him. He wasn't thinking of Yonatan and his grandfather as he should have been. For the moment he had completely forgotten about them and how worried they would be to find him gone. That was the trouble with K'tonton. It was nothing for him to remember things that had happened a thousand years ago, but he was always forgetting things that had happened a few hours ago—like promising Hannah not to leave Grandpa Ya'akov for one minute. Now as the boys and girls climbed into their open truck, all K'tonton's thoughts were of Ramat Rahel.

The boys and girls stood in the court before the dining hall of Ramat Rahel, looking up at a statue of Rachel of the Bible. She stood on a pedestal, her arms outstretched in welcome. Together they read the inscription on the base:

Thy children shall come again to their border.

The words reminded K'tonton of an old, old story about Rachel's Tomb. The story said that people passing it sometimes heard a sound of weeping—Rachel weeping for her children, who had been driven from their land. K'tonton knew that Rachel's children were the Jewish people. The inscription on the statue were the words of comfort God spoke to her, "Do not weep, Rachel. Your children shall return to their land. They shall come again to their border."

K'tonton could see the border just beyond the buildings. But it wasn't the old border of the Bible days. It was the new barbed wire border that cut the Land of Israel in two. On one side was the State of Israel, on the other side Jordan. Jordan belonged to the Arabs. Jews weren't allowed to cross over.

Zev, Miriam, Ari with K'tonton on his canteen, all the group stood solemnly before the barbed wire fence.

The leader pointed to a dusty road that wound through the hills.

"Do you see that town in the distance? It is Bethlehem where King David was born. Rachel's Tomb is on the same road—before you get to the town. By the time you grow up, the border may be open and you'll be able to visit it."

"That's too long to wait!" The words burst from Miriam's lips. She tossed her braids angrily. K'tonton could see a tear running down her cheek.

"It *is* too long to wait," he thought unhappily. "Maybe Mother Rachel doesn't know that her children have returned. Maybe she's still weeping. *Somebody* ought to tell her."

It was then that the big thought came to him. "*I* could tell her. I could slip under the fence and go to Rachel's Tomb. I'm so small the Arab guard wouldn't notice me. Maybe that's what the donkey meant when it said, 'Serve with your littleness.' "

K'tonton was already sliding from the canteen to the ground. Under the fence he squeezed, being careful not to get his jacket caught in a barb. Then he set off down the road.

Back in the truck Ari looked down at his canteen. The puppet was gone.

"What did you do with that puppet of yours, Zev?" he said.

"What puppet?" asked Zev.

"You know what puppet. The thumb-sized one that talked. It was right here on my canteen. Miriam saw it."

Zev shrugged his shoulders.

"All right. Then it wasn't a puppet. It was a real boy four inches high," said Ari sarcastically.

Everybody laughed.

"Look at that innocent look on Zev's face," they said. "He's not only a puppeteer and ventriloquist. He's an actor."

Mother Rachel Is Comforted

K'TONTON, trudging through the dust, wondered how many steps he had taken since he slipped under the wire at Ramat Raḥel. He had an uncomfortable feeling that he might not be going in the right direction.

He was sitting on a small stone beside the road, when a bearded priest in a long black gown came along. The hem of the gown brushed over K'tonton as he passed. K'tonton grabbed hold of it to keep from being swept into the dust. On went the priest with quick long strides, not knowing that a tiny person was hanging on behind. K'tonton could have jumped off if he had wanted to. But he didn't want to. He was making much better time by hanging on. Only when they reached a cluster of Arab houses, did K'tonton slide to the ground. He thought that he had come to Rachel's Tomb. But there was no tomb among the square stone houses that loomed before him. This was an Arab village close to the border. Again there was the barbed wire fence. A fierce-looking Arab with a gun stood guard.

Panic took hold of K'tonton. For a moment, he considered slipping back under the wire. Then he'd be safe in Israel. K'tonton put the thought firmly aside. He had set out to comfort Mother Rachel. If the guard stopped him, he would say boldly, "*Ivri Anokhi.* I am a Hebrew, and I am going to visit our Mother's Tomb."

But the guard was looking across the border, not down. K'tonton passed, unnoticed.

Maaaa! Clink, clank!

The sounds caught K'tonton's ear. A milkman, driving five long-eared goats before him, was going his rounds. The clanking came from a tin pail, hung by a rope from a belt around his waist. Arab children followed, laughing and chattering. K'tonton wished that he could speak to them. They didn't look like enemies. He remembered that the Arabs were Children of Ishmael, Father Abraham's son.

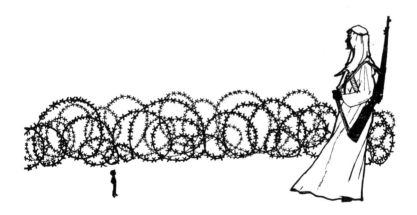

They were his cousins.

"*Halib!* Milk!" a woman called from a doorway, the last one in the village. The man stooped beside the brown-eared goat and began milking her. K'tonton had seen cows milked, but never a goat. He drew nearer to watch, his head turned up, his mouth opened wide with interest.

Squirt! A thin stream of milk landed on his head. But K'tonton didn't mind because a trickle of it got into his mouth. He swallowed it gratefully. He had not realized how dry and thirsty he was.

Now the milkman emptied his can into the woman's jar, while they spoke together in Arabic. K'tonton understood one word, *Betlehem.*

"He's going to Bethlehem," he thought. "Rachel's Tomb is on the way to Bethlehem. I could hitch a ride in his can. I don't suppose he'd mind. He has a kind face."

K'tonton considered asking the man's permission, then remembered that he was on the wrong side of the border. So he decided he'd better just hop in.

The can was leaning against a round stone that cropped out of the ground. K'tonton ran up one side of the stone and slid down the other side, landing in the bottom of the can.

"*Yallah!* Get on with you!" called the milkman.

The goats stopped nibbling the weeds. They were on their way.

The can swayed back and forth. When it dipped, K'tonton caught glimpses of hills and fields. Now a bright red poppy came into view; now a bird singing on a thistle. When the can rose, he saw only blue sky. Up, down! Up, down! Up, down!

K'tonton was beginning to wonder whether he might be on the wrong road, after all, when the can dipped once more. There beside the road was Rachel's Tomb. K'tonton knew it at once. It looked exactly like the picture in his father's book with the olive-wood covers: a square stone building with a dome on top and an open court in front. Even the tree across the road was like the one in the picture.

The milkman gathered his goats about him and sat down under the tree to rest. K'tonton slipped down the inside of the can to the ground.

Dusk was falling. A breeze stirred the leaves of the trees. The milkman and his goats had moved on.

K'tonton stood in the doorway of the tomb, listening. Was it a sound of weeping that he heard? Or was it a sigh, a deep sigh like his mother's, the day she thought he had been lost? Words of comfort tumbled from K'tonton's lips.

"I have come to bring you good news, Mother Rachel. Your children have returned to their borders—Shimshon and Hannah and Raphael and Shalom—all the *olim*."

The words came faster in a singing, chanting tone:

> "*They plant vineyards and eat thereof:*
> *They plant in the wilderness*
> *The cedar and acacia, the myrtle and*
>   *the oleaster . . .*

also the tamarisk and eucalyptus . . . and fig trees and olive trees . . . and orange trees. Banana trees, too. Shimshon says so."

K'tonton paused and listened anxiously. Again he heard the sighing. Maybe Mother Rachel was wondering why her children did not come to her.

"It is because there is a border with barbed wire," K'tonton explained earnestly. "The Arabs—they are children of Ishmael—do not let them pass. Only I, because of my littleness, could come. But soon there will be peace and *all* will come to you."

Again K'tonton listened. The sighing in the tomb had passed away. K'tonton himself breathed a sigh, a little sigh of relief. Mother Rachel had been comforted.

Now that he had finished his errand, K'tonton remembered how hungry he was. Except for the mouthful of goat's milk, he had had nothing to eat or drink since morning. A fountain stood nearby. It was too high for K'tonton to reach; but a trickle of water had run down, filling a little hollow in a stone below. K'tonton cupped the water in his hands and drank.

Now what could he do for food? He thrust his hands into his pockets to think. K'tonton always thought better when his hands were clasped behind his back or thrust into his pockets. His fingers brushed against something. Two sunflower seeds! They must have gotten into his pocket the day he fell into Shalom's mother's bag. Gratefully, K'tonton recited a blessing, cracked open a sunflower seed, and ate.

Night had fallen. Moonlight silvered the blackness. K'tonton found a little opening between the stones of the wall, crept inside and slept. A smile played on his lips. He was dreaming of Mother Rachel, comforted at last. In his dream her face was like his mother's.

The sun had just risen when K'tonton awoke. He heard voices speaking Arabic. A man, riding on a small brown donkey, stopped in the road. Behind him walked two Arab women, carrying baskets of vegetables on their heads. The younger woman set down her basket and knelt near Rachel's Tomb. Her lips moved in prayer.

"*Tai!* Come along!" The man spoke quickly, motioning to her to hurry.

Again K'tonton caught a name, *Il Kuds*. Shimshon had once told him that this was the Arab name for Jerusalem.

"They're on their way to Jerusalem—the Arab part, inside the walls," K'tonton thought excitedly. "If I go along, I'll get inside too. I'll see the *Kotel Hama'aravi*, the wall of the Holy Temple."

Quickly K'tonton washed his hands in dew, then raced to the basket. He had just climbed over the side and crouched down behind a head of lettuce, when the woman stooped and lifted the basket to her head. They were on their way; the man on his donkey, the women on foot, single file, carrying the baskets of vegetables on their heads, and K'tonton, high up in the second basket, reciting his morning prayers:

> *Glorify the Lord, O Jerusalem!*
> *Praise the Lord, O Zion!*

Adventure in the Old City

K'TONTON, peeking out from beneath a bunch of scallions, saw high walls loom up before him. They were outside the gates of Jerusalem. People shouted and jostled. Someone from the city was bargaining with the Arab on the donkey. K'tonton found himself tumbling from the basket into a handcart. Radishes, cucumbers, onions rolling around him. Through the gate the cart trundled, jolting over rough cobblestones. They were in a noisy, roofed-over street. All around them were shops. Only they didn't look like shops. They looked like openings in the wall. K'tonton saw vegetables, cereals, sides of mutton, clay pots, copper pots, jewelry, bolts of cloth, baskets, donkey harnesses, souvenirs. They were piled on the floors in sacks and in baskets, hung from ceilings and walls. People were fingering and squeezing the things, talking loudly to the shopkeepers as if they were angry. But they weren't really angry, because afterward they paid their money and took their goods and looked pleased.

Two eyes weren't enough for K'tonton to see all he wanted to see. "But one nose is too many," he thought, holding his nose with two fingers to keep out the smells—rotting fruit and donkey droppings, and cooking mutton. Then he dropped his fingers and sniffed. A new spicy smell was coming toward him. It made K'tonton think of the incense burned in the Holy Temple: balm and frankincense and myrrh, cassia, spikenard and saffron.

Soon he, K'tonton, would be standing in the Holy Temple—not exactly in the Temple, but before a *wall* of the Temple, the western wall. "How pleased Father will be when I write him that I've prayed at the *Kotel Hama'-aravi*," K'tonton thought.

But before he could reach the western wall, something unexpected happened.

It began when K'tonton noticed a camel going round and round in a circle, a sad-looking camel, its eyes blindfolded. It was turning the stones of an olive press. Oil from the olives ran out of a funnel into a stone basin.

K'tonton slid down the cart of vegetables and drew nearer to watch. A group of tourists was also watching. K'tonton could tell they were tourists by their sunglasses and the cameras that hung from their shoulders. A man was talking to them. He spoke in English, but he wore a *kaffia*, an Arab head scarf, so K'tonton knew that he was an Arab.

The man was saying, "From the balcony of my hotel, I

can see my house in Katamon, but I can't go to it. *They* live there now."

"Katamon! That's the place where Shimshon's grandmother lives," K'tonton thought. "Maybe it's this man's house she lives in."

K'tonton knew that Shimshon's grandmother used to live in the Old City near the western wall. But the war came and Arab soldiers blew up her house, so she had to find a new place to live.

K'tonton felt that he had to explain. "Sir," he said, raising his voice high, so that the man might hear. "Shimshon's grandmother didn't want to go to your house. She wanted to stay in her own house. She too, is sad,—for her house, and because she cannot pray at the wall of the Holy Temple."

The man turned angrily to see where the voice was coming from. This way, he looked, that way, and behind him—but not down. K'tonton saw his face turn purple.

"Come out, you brazen one with the voice of a mouse," he shouted. "I'll wipe you off the earth."

K'tonton flattened himself against a wall, hoping that he wouldn't be noticed among the shadows.

"Phone the police! Warn the border guard!" the man shouted. "There's a spy inside the walls."

"Spy! A spy in the city! Stop him! Catch him! That's the way he went. No, that way!"

People were running and screaming and pointing.

K'tonton raced along the gutter, slipping over peelings, stumbling over the rough cobblestones. The street narrowed. Baskets heaped with spices stood in all the stalls. This was where the sweet smell had come from. K'tonton climbed into a basket of cloves, his heart thumping.

"Nobody will think of looking for me here," he thought, as he burrowed into the spices. "I'll be safe."

He lifted his eyes above the rim of the basket and glanced toward the street to make sure.

A ragged urchin was pointing straight toward him.

"There he is," the boy cried. "I saw him go in."

"Where?" The angry man had come up.

"There," said the boy again.

"Stupid! You see a mouse!" said the man, and ran on.

K'tonton waited until the shouts had died away. Then he crept cautiously out of the spice heap and turned back in the direction from which he had come. Now he hid behind a basket. Now he darted from one basket to the next. Now he crept through a hole in a partition. He was back in the wide market from which he had come. Around him were souvenirs, charms, jewelry, donkey harnesses embroidered in black and red, camel bells. Someone was coming near. K'tonton hid quickly under a brass bell.

"Mary," said a woman's voice, "what about buying this donkey harness? It would be an interesting thing to show in class."

"But the weight of it, Agnes!" said a second voice. "Remember we're going back by plane. Forty-four pounds of luggage is all we can take. The children would be just as interested in one of these bells."

The bell over K'tonton was lifted. Two women were

looking down at him, their eyes wide with surprise.

"You couldn't be . . . you're not Tom Thumb, are you?" asked the older woman.

"No," said K'tonton politely. "I'm K'tonton."

"Maybe he's Thumbelina's brother," said the younger woman.

"I have no brother or sister," K'tonton explained. He looked up at the women. They were Americans. He could tell by the way they talked. Probably they were teachers. They had spoken about a class. The older one—the other had called her Agnes—had smile wrinkles under her eyes. K'tonton felt sure that he could trust her.

"I—I'm the one everybody is chasing," he confessed.

"You!"

The women looked K'tonton over from head to foot, all four inches.

The older one laughed loud. "*You*, the dangerous spy!"

K'tonton didn't know why she was laughing, but it was a pleasant laugh. So he laughed with her—until he remembered that he had better explain.

"I'm *not* a spy," he said. "I just wanted to see the *Kotel Hama'aravi*. That's the wall of the Holy Temple."

"Of course you wanted to see your holy places," said the woman. "We've just come from ours." A glance passed between her and the younger woman. "The Wailing Wall is our next stop. We particularly asked to see it. We could take you with us. What did you say your name was?"

"K'tonton."

"You may call me Miss Agnes, Tom Tom, and this is Miss Mary."

A guide was coming toward them. Miss Agnes screened K'tonton with her hand.

"Abdul," said Miss Mary, "we're taking this bell and the nose ring and bracelet. Come and help me bargain with the shopkeeper."

The two walked off.

"Quick!" Miss Agnes said, handing K'tonton a tissue. "Wipe off your shoes and get into my pocket." She held out the jacket she was carrying on her arm.

"H'm," she said, sniffing as K'tonton hopped in. "Where have you been? You smell like the Queen of Sheba in all her glory."

Treasure

THE street went down and down and down. It was more like a staircase than a street, narrow, with rough stone stairs and houses like straight walls on each side. Black shadows fell across the walls. K'tonton was glad that he was safe in Miss Agnes's pocket.

Suddenly the stairs came to an end. They were in a wide, open court. A towering wall made of huge stones rose before them. K'tonton climbed out of Miss Agnes's pocket and ran to it. This was the *Kotel Hama'aravi*, the wall of the Holy Temple—the western wall that God had said would never be destroyed. K'tonton pressed a cheek against the rough stone, then touched it with his lips.

From the far end of the court came the voice of the guide. "This is the Wailing Wall, the remains of the foundation of King Solomon's Temple. For thousands of years Jews have prayed and wept before this wall. They would write out prayers and stick them into the cracks between the rocks."

K'tonton wiped a tear out of his own eyes, and began swaying in prayer.

> *Oh, turn in loving kindness to Jerusalem!*
> *May peace and joy abide in Jerusalem!*

"Amen," said a voice behind him. It was Miss Agnes who spoke.

"Miss Agnes," K'tonton asked, "do you have a piece of paper you can spare? I want to write a prayer."

He took from his pocket the bit of lead he always carried there. Miss Agnes tore a sheet out of her notebook, then stooped, holding the book out for K'tonton to lean on.

In thin spidery letters K'tonton wrote the prayer that had been in his heart since he crossed the border the day before.

> *Please, God, let the Children of Israel and the*
> *Children of Ishmael be friends.*

"Maybe I ought to use some words out of the prayer book," he thought, and wrote on:

> *For the sake of Abraham our Father, speedily in*
> *our day.*

He folded the paper and stuck it into a crack in the wall.

"Get back into my pocket, Tomtom. The guide is leaving," said Miss Agnes.

Back they went, up the steep stairs. K'tonton wondered where Shimshon's grandmother had lived. He wondered where all the synagogues were, the ones whose pictures were in the book with the olive-wood covers. They had reached the first arch over the street, when K'tonton noticed at one side a court filled with stones and rubble. Broken stairs led up to it.

"Maybe *this* was a synagogue," K'tonton thought. "I'd better take a look."

One leg was already out of the jacket pocket. "I have to see something, Miss Agnes. I'll be right back," he called, and slid to the ground without waiting for an answer.

Now he was inside the opening. He dug his heels in the rubble beside the stairs and began inching his way up, sometimes upright, sometimes on his hands and knees. He was in the court at last. Something glinted on the ground before him, something made of silver—a tiny, pointing finger. K'tonton stooped and began digging around it with a bit of stone. Three more fingers appeared, folded over a thumb. It was a *yad*, a pointer, shaped like a hand, the kind used in the synagogue to point to the letters when the Torah scroll is read. The tiny hand was perfect. Only the part above the wrist had been broken off.

"I'll take it back with me," K'tonton told himself, his heart thumping with excitement. "It's lucky that I came."

But *how* could he carry it back? Tiny as the *yad* was, it was almost as big as he was.

"If I had strong thread or a cord, I could bind it to my back," K'tonton thought. "You can carry heavy loads on your back."

But he didn't have a cord. Suddenly K'tonton felt very tired, very helpless and alone.

"Please, God, help me," he prayed. "I can't leave the *yad* here by itself. I *have* to take it back with me." And K'tonton looked anxiously at the tiny pointer lying forlornly at his feet.

It was then that he noticed the fringes. They were lying in the dust, attached to a torn-off corner of a prayer shawl, a *tallit*.

K'tonton picked up the fringes and kissed them, his heart trembling. God had answered his prayer. The fringes were the answer. He could use them to bind the *yad* to his back. Quickly he divided the thread into two parts. Three threads he wound around the pointing finger, the remaining four around the wrist. Straining and tugging, he lifted the pointer to his back. Then he brought the ends of the fringes under his arms and around his waist, and knotted them securely. Slipping and sliding, but always careful not to hurt the precious *yad*, K'tonton made his way to the street.

The party of tourists had reached the last of the stairs, when Miss Agnes happened to look down into her jacket pocket.

"Mary," she said, "the little fellow, TomTom, he's gone!"

They searched in the folds of the jacket, in the second pocket, on the pavement. K'tonton wasn't to be found.

"When did you see him last?" Mary asked.

"Just before we came to that first arch," Miss Agnes answered.

Suddenly she remembered hearing K'tonton say something about having to go somewhere—he'd be right back. At that moment she had been too busy watching the sights to more than half hear. Now everything returned to her.

"I'm going back for him," she said.

"But, sister," Mary protested, "we can't go back by ourselves."

"I'm going," said Agnes firmly. "I couldn't live with myself if I left that little one behind."

"Can I help you? Have you lost something?" The guide had come up.

Miss Agnes nodded, but she didn't tell him *what* she had lost.

"We have to go back a piece," she explained, "but we don't want to hold up the party. Can you get someone to go with us? We'll catch up with you at the gate."

The guide spoke to a young boy in Arabic. The boy, followed by the two women, returned down the steep stairs. Miss Agnes's anxious eyes searched the pavement, the shadows. They reached the last arch.

"Miss Agnes! Miss Agnes!" The thin excited voice came from an opening at one side.

"Distract the boy's attention," Agnes whispered to Mary.

Mary stopped and began asking questions. Miss Agnes hurried to the opening in the wall. K'tonton was sliding down the rubble. His clothes were torn. He was covered with dust, but his eyes were shining. Something as big as he was, was bound to his back.

"Miss Agnes, Miss Agnes!" he cried. "Look what I found. A pointer . . . for a *Sefer Torah*. I'm taking it back . . ."

"Into my pocket! Quick!" said Miss Agnes. "You'll tell me about it later."

This time she didn't wait for him to wipe off the dust. She grabbed him in her hand and stuck him deep into her pocket.

"I've found what I was looking for," she called to the Arab boy. "We can turn back."

Outside the Mandelbaum Gate, on the Israeli side of the border, drivers waited for the tourists passing through from Jordan. Shimshon was among them. A shrill cry startled him.

"Shimshon! There's Shimshon."

For a moment Shimshon thought that he had imagined the voice. Since Grandpa Ya'akov had reported K'tonton's disappearance the day before, the little one had been constantly on his mind.

But it wasn't Shimshon's imagination. Two tourists were coming toward him, one with her hand outstretched. K'tonton was standing on it. His hair was sticky, his cheeks smeared with dust, his knees bruised. His clothes smelled faintly of spices. Something on his back rose high above his head.

"It can't be!" Shimshon thought. "But it is—a *yad!*"

The women had come up to him.

"TomTom says you're the friend he lives with. I'm so glad you are here," said the older one, handing K'tonton to Shimshon. "It's a relief to put him into safe hands— though I don't know why I should have worried about the child. There's a special Providence watching over him."

"Look up, K'tonton! Smile!" said the younger woman, as she focused a camera on him.

"There's our guide! We're going on to Nazareth," said the elder. "*Shalom,* TomTom."

She threw him a kiss and the two walked away.

Shimshon heard the elder say to the younger, "This is one experience we won't talk about. Folks at home would think we'd been touched by the sun—even *with* the picture."

From K'tonton's letter to his Father and Mother:

> *So now the* yad *is safe. Shimshon's grandmother cried when she saw it. Hannah said not to mind, she was crying from happiness. Grandpa Ya'-akov says he forgives me for running off and giving him such a hard time.*
>
> *At first they wanted me to give the* yad *to the museum. But you have taught me that a lost object that is found must be returned to its owner. So I told Shimshon. Shimshon said, "The people from the Old City are the owners. We will give the* yad *to their synagogue in Katamon."*
>
> *Now Yedidya's father is making a new handle and chain for the* yad. *He is very skilled with silver and gold and brass.*
>
> *I think the* yad *will be glad to point to the holy letters again.*
>
> *From me, your loving son,*
K'tonton
>
> *P.S. I found your letter when I came back. Do not worry, Mother. I will not cross the border again. But it is lucky I went this time on account of the* yad.

A Job in a Tree Nursery

HANNAH picked up the bit of material on which she had been working. She was making a knapsack, the kind that scouts carry on hikes. But this one was very tiny.

"It's for K'tonton," she explained to Shimshon. "Yedidya's father is making him a canteen. I want to be sure that he has a supply of food and water the next time he wanders off."

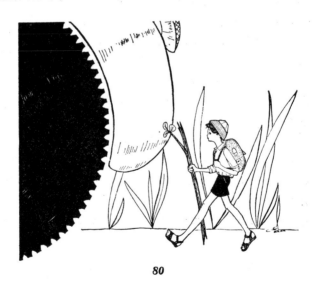

She showed Shimshon two sets of tiny dishes for the knapsack, one for dairy foods, one for meat. There were a cup, plate, knife, fork and spoon in each.

"I bought them in a toy store," she said. "Even there it was hard to get them small enough."

"Don't you think the knapsack will put ideas into K'ton-ton's head?" Shimshon asked. "First thing you know he'll be wanting to go off."

"The idea is in his head already," said Hannah. "Yesterday he began telling me how Abraham, our Father, walked the length and breadth of the land from Dan to Beersheba. He wanted to know where Dan and Beersheba were. And this morning he told me he didn't think he was needed in the Clinic any more. He said, "There is a new nurse there who makes the children laugh, even without somersaults."

Shimshon smiled. "The child is restless. I have to go down to Natanya tomorrow. I'll take him with me."

Early the next morning Shimshon started out with K'tonton, but K'tonton wasn't with him when he returned!

"I left the child for just a minute—on a bench near the railway stop," Shimshon explained to Hannah. "When the train pulled out, he was gone."

Hannah didn't say, "I told you so." She just said, "I'm glad he had his knapsack and canteen." Then she sighed, "I wonder what the little one is up to now?"

K'tonton wasn't up to anything. Leaving Shimshon was a pure accident. He had been waiting for Shimshon near the train stop in Natanya, when a farmer drove up in a wagon with rubber-tire wheels. Running beside his horse was a little colt. The colt was tied to his mother by a long rope. When the wagon came to a stop, the colt snuggled against his mother. His head just fitted under her neck.

A dreadful feeling of homesickness came over K'tonton as he watched. For a moment he wished that *his* mother had tied him to her with a string. Then he wouldn't be so far away, with two seas between him and his parents. Something salty rolled down on K'tonton's lip. It was a tear. More tears fell.

K'tonton scolded himself severely. "You ought to be ashamed of yourself, K'tonton, crying like a baby. What would Shimshon think if he saw you?"

To make sure that Shimshon didn't see him until he had

gotten over his crying, K'tonton crept into a bouquet of flowers that someone had set down on the bench.

Too-oo-oo Too-oo-oo. K'tonton heard the whistle of a train, a screech of brakes. Wheels ground to a stop. Someone picked up the bouquet of flowers with K'tonton inside, and boarded the train.

"All aboard! Next stop Hedera!"

The train was on its way.

K'tonton, peeking out from the bouquet of flowers, saw that he was on the back of a seat in a small compartment. Two long benches faced each other. Through the window sand dunes, meadows, orchards, flew by. Three goats, chewing weeds near the tracks, raced off in a panic. A row of geese paraded slowly across a field.

The young man in the seat below K'tonton—the one without a hat—had taken a book out of his pocket. He looked out of the window, read in the book, looked out of the window, turned to another page in the book.

K'tonton decided it must be a guide book. But when he glanced down, he saw that the book was a *Tanakh*, a Hebrew Bible. Now a new sound caught K'tonton's ear. The man at the end of the bench—an old bearded man—had also opened a book and begun reading—not silently like the young man, but in soft singing tones. K'tonton's homesickness rushed back. This was how his father studied Torah. K'tonton edged nearer, along the back of the bench, to listen.

The old man glanced up. A troubled look came into his eyes. "I'm seeing what can't be there," he was thinking. "It must be my age. Can my mind be growing confused?"

Then he remembered that long ago when he was a little child, his mother had told him about a tiny boy named Fingerel, who had saved his brothers and sisters from the belly of a bear. The old man also remembered that the great writer Agnon had once written about a tiny rabbi, Rabbi Gadiel by name, even smaller than a finger. If his mother and the wise Agnon had said there were tiny people in the world, surely he could believe his own eyes.

"*Shalom*," he said to K'tonton.

"*Shalom*," said K'tonton. "You study just like my father."

"And who is your father?" the old man asked.

"He's Baruch Reuben," K'tonton answered. "I'm Isaac Samuel ben Baruch Reuben, but they call me K'tonton."

The old man smiled. "I think I'll call you Pintele— Pintele Yid," he said. "You can call me Zaydeh. I'd like to be grandfather to a little grandson like you."

At this point the young man raised his eyes from the Bible. He looked queerly at the old man, as if he thought he was talking to himself. So they didn't say any more until the young man got out at Hedera.

Then K'tonton poured out his whole story: how he had

left his father and mother to come up to the Land of Israel;
how he had met Hannah and Raphael and Shimshon, and
about the homesick spell he had had when he saw the little
colt with his mother.

Through the window K'tonton caught a glimpse of an
orange grove. It reminded him of the little grove his father
had planted for him in a window box at home.

"I took good care of the trees," K'tonton said. "I pretended they were growing in the Land of Israel."

"How would you like to tend to trees that are really
growing in Israel?" the old man asked.

K'tonton's eyes filled with eagerness. "Could I?" he
asked.

"If you went home with me, you could," said Zaydeh. "It
just happens that I work in a tree nursery. That's where you
plant baby trees."

Then he told K'tonton about the kibbutz—the settlement where he lived—and the tiny baby trees that had to be
tended carefully until they were big enough to be trans-
planted into new forests.

"You'd be just the right size to look after them, Pintele,"
he said. "You wouldn't have to bend over double the way I
do. What do you say? Will you come and help me? I'm
getting off at the next stop."

The happiness in K'tonton's eyes told him that the answer was "Yes."

Dear Shimshon:

I did not mean to leave you, but I was in a bouquet of flowers, and the man took it on the train. So now I am in a kibbutz with the Zaydeh. He calls me Pintele . . . I guess because I'm so small. I met him on the train. We work in the nursery where the baby trees grow. He says I am a great help. That's because he has the rheumatism and it's hard for him to bend, but I am just the right size. I will make you a picture of our trees.

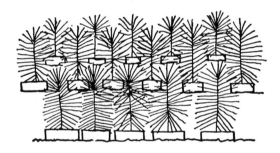

These are kerosene cans, eight rows, very long ones. You cut the can in half and drill holes in the corners and put in earth and plant ten seeds in each one. I did not draw the seeds because you could not see them in the ground, but you can see the baby pine trees. Soon they will grow big enough to plant on the hills, and there will be a

new forest. *Zaydeh says some day he will take me in a jeep to see the new forests, also the old ones.*

I would like to grow big like my trees. But Zaydeh says it is good that I am small because, before I came, he had to bend double to reach the inside rows. Now I weed them. You cannot find one weed in my cans.

If there is a letter from my father and mother, will you send it to me, please? The reason I got into the bouquet of flowers was that I was lonesome for them. I am lonesome for you too, especially Raphael. After a while, I will come to see you.

Todah rabbah! *Thank you very much.*

Your loving friend,
K'tonton

A Lizard Helps K'tonton Find Water

No one in the kibbutz knew about K'tonton, except the old grandfather. The house where the children lived was far from the tree nursery, and the workers were grownups. Grownups seldom noticed K'tonton, even when he was right under their noses—unless someone called their attention to him, which Zaydeh never did.

"When you get to be my age, people think you imagine things," he explained to K'tonton. "It's better to let them discover you by themselves."

But no one *did* discover K'tonton until one day, when Zaydeh was sprinkling the seedlings at the far end of the rows. K'tonton was hoeing the ground under the ten-inch trees. Suddenly he had a feeling that someone was watching him. He looked up.

A boy with big solemn eyes was staring at him. The boy

was about his own age but not, of course, his size. He didn't smile. He didn't speak. He just stared.

"He's looking at my trees," K'tonton thought. "He's surprised to see how green they are."

K'tonton himself was so interested in the trees, he thought that everyone must feel as he did. He called out, "There's a path down the middle of the rows, if you want to come closer."

The boy started in surprise. He hadn't expected so tiny a person to speak. "Excuse me!" he said. "It isn't polite to stare, but I never saw anyone your size before."

"I'm the only one—so far as I know," said K'tonton. "I'm K'tonton, but Zaydeh calls me Pintele. What's your name?"

"Yosef," said the boy. "I live in the village." He pointed into the distance, where two rows of small white houses stood out against a hillside.

"That's where our trees are going when they get big enough," K'tonton said excitedly. "Right on top of your hill—to start a new forest."

"I know," said the boy. "My father is up there now, breaking the rocks, so the trees can be planted. The Jewish National Fund gave him a job . . . until our own land is ready."

"Zaydeh says the kibbutz people worked for the Jewish National Fund until *their* land was ready. They started the tree nursery. Now most of the workers in the nursery come from the new villages. Are you one of the *olim?*"

Yosef answered that he was. "They didn't want us where we were, so we came here," he said. "My father says that in Israel they want us. Didn't they want you where *you* were?"

K'tonton explained that he was a visitor from America. "I came to see Israel," he said, "but now I'm helping. There's a lot of work to do here."

He bent over and pulled the tiny beginning of a weed from under a tree.

Yosef stooped to lift a heavy pail at his side. It was full of water.

"I have to go now or my mother will scold me," he said.

90

"She's waiting for the water. She'll scold me, anyway," he added, " 'cause half the water will be gone when I get home. I filled the pail full up. You can see for yourself. But the water splashes out on the way."

Again he stared at K'tonton, as if he were afraid the tiny fellow would disappear when he turned his back.

"Do you work here every day?" he asked.

"Except Shabbat," K'tonton answered. I only *look* at the trees on Shabbat."

"Then I'll see you tomorrow," said Yosef. He turned and set out toward the village. At every rough place in the road, water splashed out of the pail.

After this, almost every day, Yosef stopped near the rows of trees where K'tonton was at work, set down his pail, and visited with him. Soon K'tonton knew all about Yosef and his family. In the land where they used to live, all their belongings had been taken from them and they had had to leave their home. Then a big ship brought them to Israel. Now they had a home in the new village on the hill. Everything they needed was waiting for them when they came— beds, chairs, a table, pots and dishes, a kerosene stove, a sink and a shower with pipes, but no water in the pipes. The village didn't have a well—just a cistern to catch rain water. When his mother wanted extra water, he had to fetch it for her from the *kibbutz*. But soon, Yosef said, they would have their own well. The government men said so.

Yosef was always talking about that well. "When our village gets the new well," he would say, "water will run right through a pipe into our kitchen," or, "My father is going to plant fruit trees and a vegetable garden and peanuts and sunflowers when we get our new well. I'll give you some of the seeds."

Once Zaydeh picked a rose for Yosef to take home to his mother. "When we get our new well," Yosef said, "I'll plant a whole rose bush for her, and grass in front of our house, just like in the *kibbutz*."

Until Yosef came, K'tonton hadn't thought much about water. There was no need for him to think about it. When he had wanted water, he had turned a faucet and got it. Now he, too, began dreaming about water almost as much as Yosef did.

"Zaydeh," he asked, "if they don't get water in the village, how will they plant the trees? Baby trees need water."

Zaydeh saw the worry line in K'tonton's forehead. "But they *will* get water," he assured him. "The government wouldn't have built the village if it didn't know there was water there."

"But Yosef said they drilled and no water came."

"The well drillers will be back to try again," Zaydeh said. "When they come, we'll go up to the village to watch them. How would you like that, Pintele?"

K'tonton's smile told Zaydeh he would like it very much.

A day came when Yosef brought exciting news. A crew of well drillers had arrived in the village. The machinery was already set up and the work had begun.

Zaydeh kept his promise. On Friday, when work in the tree nursery stopped at noon, he walked over to the village,

K'tonton on his shoulder. From below came the thud, thud of the drill. Zaydeh stopped under an old olive tree and looked down. All the children of the village, and many of the grownups were watching the well drillers at work. A tall tripod had been set up with a pulley at the top. Through the pulley ran a long rope. A heavy pounder at the end weighed it down. Below the pounder was a length of pipe, partly in the ground.

The men pulled at the rope. Up rose the heavy pounder. The men dropped the rope. Down on the pipe came the pounder, pushing it deeper into the rock.

Zaydeh explained that the pounder had a drill, a sharp-pointed rod that went down through the pipe.

Pull'l'l! Drop! Thud! Pull'l'l! Drop! Thud!

The drill bit deeper and deeper into the rock.

Zaydeh sat down under the olive tree to rest. K'tonton slid down his arm to a root sticking out of the ground. Where the root ended, he found a ledge with a better view.

Listening to the chug of the motor, the thud of the drill, K'tonton dreamed about the stream of water that would soon rise. It would run through pipes into Yosef's mother's kitchen to wash the dishes and the clothes. Yosef would get no more scoldings because his pail was half full. Water would splash from the shower head onto Yosef's father and brothers when they came in from the fields, hot and sweaty. It would sprinkle like rain on rows of onions and cucumbers and eggplants. Full pails would water the plum trees and the baby pines on the hill.

"Where's K'tonton?"

93

It was Yosef who spoke. He had spied Zaydeh and came running up the hill.

Zaydeh pointed to the ledge.

"My father said they've gone down fifty feet," Yosef announced. "They'll test for water any minute. May I take K'tonton with me?"

"No," said Zaydeh. "He's safer here with me."

"See you later, K'tonton!" Yosef waved, and was off.

The sputt-tt of the motor, the thud of the drill stopped. K'tonton watched carefully. The foreman had taken a coil of rope with a sinker attached, and was lowering it into the pipe. Down, down, down went the rope. Now the foreman began drawing the rope up again. No one in the crowd spoke. All eyes were on the rope. If the end of the rope came up wet, they would know that they had reached water.

Zaydeh had explained all this to K'tonton. It seemed to him now that he had never wanted anything so much as to see that rope-end come up wet. But it *didn't* come up wet.

"Bone dry!" said the foreman.

"Only Elijah the Prophet can help us now," someone in the crowd exclaimed.

"Maybe Elijah *will* help."

The second voice didn't come from below. Whoever had spoken was close at hand.

K'tonton turned quickly. Behind him stood an old man he hadn't noticed before. The man, even older than Zaydeh, had a long white beard. He carried a staff in his hand, but he didn't lean on it. He stood straight and tall.

It was at that moment that K'tonton noticed the lizard. It was lying on a rock below him, sunning itself. K'tonton had seen many lizards since coming to Israel—streaking up a garden wall, or running along an overhanging ledge, sometimes upside down like a fly. He had often wondered how they managed to hold on. But lizards move with unbelievable speed, so that K'tonton had never been able to find out. Now a lizard was lying perfectly still on a rock below him. Worried as he was about the water, K'tonton couldn't help leaning over to get a better look.

Maybe the ledge was more crumbly than K'tonton thought. Maybe he leaned over too far. Down K'tonton went, turned a flip-flop in the air, and landed face down on the lizard's back. In a flash the lizard was off, carrying K'tonton. K'tonton flattened himself against the lizard and held on with both hands. He expected to be thrown off at any moment. But the lizard didn't seem to notice that it had a rider. Along the rocky ledge it sped, through brush and tangled vines, to a crack where a clump of bell-like flowers grew out of the rock. There it headed down a straight rock wall. *Click, click, click* went the lizard's feet. K'tonton, riding head down, could see how the lizard clung to the rocks. It had a tiny pad like a suction cup on each foot.

Now K'tonton noticed something unusual about the rocks. They didn't look like the ledges on the hillside. These stones looked even, as if someone had laid them one atop the other. Could this be an old wall that somebody had made?

A small stone loosened as they passed, and went whizzing down. Plop! The sound came from far below. The splash of water!

"But it can't be water," K'tonton told himself. "I've been thinking so much about water, I must have imagined it."

Another stone flew past. Again K'tonton heard the *plop*. It *was* the splash of water. There was no mistaking it. Somewhere, far down in this very spot, THERE WAS WATER.

K'tonton's heart began going *plop, plop*. "I must get back to the village at once," he thought. "I must tell the people about the water . . . before the workmen leave."

But *how* was he to get back? Even if it were safe to slide off the lizard's back—which it wasn't—how could he get to the top of this straight wall? *He* didn't have pads on his feet like a lizard.

The lizard itself solved the problem. To K'tonton's amazement, it turned around and began streaking *up* the straight rocks it had just come down. Now K'tonton had to hold fast to keep from sliding down its tail. Up and up went the lizard with K'tonton on its back. Now it reached the clump of flowers that hung from the crevice. Now it ran through brush and tangled vines to the flat rock where K'tonton had first seen it. Up the side of the hill it sped. There it stopped—at the feet of the old man who had said that Elijah might come.

K'tonton hopped off the lizard's back. Before he had time to say, "thank you," the lizard had gone. K'tonton turned to speak to the old man. He too, had gone. Could the stranger have been Elijah the Prophet? Had Elijah sent the lizard to help him find water for the village? There was no time to think.

The crowd had left, but the well drillers were still there. Yosef was watching them. K'tonton raced over to Zaydeh, his feet moving almost as fast as the lizard's.

"Zaydeh," he cried, "don't let the drillers go away.

There's water here . . . deep in the rocks. That way . . . I heard it!"

Quickly he told Zaydeh what had happened. With his tiny pencil he made a rough diagram of the route: the olive trees, the rock below, the ledge overgrown with tangled vines, the plant with the bell-like flowers growing out of a crack, the stone wall going down and down.

Zaydeh hurried down to the foreman of the crew. He didn't tell him *how* he knew about the water, just that he knew. And he showed the foreman the diagram.

The foreman didn't put much faith in Zaydeh's talk, but he agreed to take a look. Carefully he made his way along the ledge of rock, sometimes stopping to cut back brush and tangled vines. Zaydeh, who was quite spry for his age when his rheumatism didn't bother him, followed with K'tonton standing in his pocket. Behind them came Yosef.

When they reached the plant growing out of the crevice, the foreman knelt down to examine the stones below. K'tonton saw a look of interest. The foreman began pushing aside fallen branches, dirt and leaves, working with both hands. As he worked, the wall grew wider, curved, formed a circle.

The foreman was on his feet. "You've found a well," he said to Zaydeh. "Probably an old crusader's well. Sometimes we discover them around here—maybe eight, nine hundred years old. They're choked up, but the water is there. Clean this out, reline the walls, put down a pipe, and with luck you'll have water."

Yosef raced back to the village with the good news.

Once more, on a Friday afternoon, Zaydeh set out for the village. This time K'tonton rode in the pocket of Zaydeh's white Sabbath shirt. The streets of the village were empty. Zaydeh followed the new path to the well. All the villagers were gathered around it, their eyes on the pump. Someone started the motor. From the pipes came a hissing of air, then a bubbling, gurgling sound. Water was gushing out of the pump—clear, pure water. It splashed on the ground. It sparkled and danced. It flowed and flowed, forming a little pool in the rocks.

"*Ma'yim!! Ma'yim!* Water!"

The villagers shook hands. They laughed and cried. The children splashed into the water, clothes and all. Some were already dressed for the Sabbath, but no one scolded them. Yosef grabbed K'tonton and let *him* feel the good water flow over him. Dripping wet, the children formed a circle, and danced and sang:

*Ma'yim, ma'yim, ma'yim, ma'yim
Ma'yim, ma'yim, besason.*

The grownups joined in the song:

*And ye shall draw water in joy
From the springs of salvation.
Water, water, water in joy.*

In Tel Aviv

K'TONTON might have stayed on in the tree nursery if it were not for the promise he had made to himself to travel through the whole land. He spoke to Zaydeh about it.

"I'll miss you, Pintele," Zaydeh said. "You have been a help and a comfort to me. But I won't try to keep you back. It is written, 'If one begins a good deed—a *mitzvah*—say to him, 'Complete it.' "

So one morning, very early, K'tonton, his knapsack and canteen hanging from his shoulders, bade Zaydeh and Yosef goodbye, and set out. There were bread and cheese in his knapsack; in the canteen, water from the well which he had helped to find.

Zaydeh had had Yosef bring the water from the village. "There is a blessing in it, Pintele," he said.

At first K'tonton tried asking for rides, but a thumb-sized person is too small to be seen from a passing car. Even drivers in parked cars seldom noticed him. So K'tonton soon got into the habit of getting into a car without waiting to be asked.

It was in this way that he arrived in Tel Aviv. The car was one of the taxis that take people from city to city, like a bus. Through the window K'tonton could see that Tel Aviv was a big, exciting city that had apartment houses, stores and hotels. Many people were getting into buses, or talking on the sidewalks, or eating at tables on the sidewalks.

Then the taxi stopped. K'tonton hopped onto a parcel a passenger was carrying. He had taken hold of it on the underside, hooking his feet through the string. Doubled up like a U, nobody noticed him.

The man walked down one street, down another street, and then turned into a park. Now K'tonton could see that Tel Aviv was on the seashore. The park had bright flower beds and little trees bent over by the wind, all in the same direction. There was a railing, and below the railing, the beach. K'tonton unhooked his feet, let go of the string, and dropped down to the sand.

Then the accident happened. A boy in a bathing suit, who hadn't noticed K'tonton, dumped a bucketful of sand over him. The more K'tonton tried to push his way out, the deeper into the sand he went. It is fun to have your body and your arms and legs buried in warm sand, but it isn't fun to have your head buried.

Goodness knows what would have become of K'tonton if a little girl with a pail and a toy sieve hadn't come along just then and scooped him up. *She* didn't know about K'tonton either, until she emptied the pail of sand into her sieve. There he was!

The little girl was too young to be surprised at K'tonton's littleness. She had always wanted a brother. Now one had come. She brushed the sand out of his hair and tidied his clothes, like a big sister. Luckily, no sand had gotten into K'tonton's eyes. This was because he had shut them tight when he had dropped into the sand. It was a habit of K'tonton's to shut his eyes whenever he jumped.

"Ilsa, it's time to go home," someone, leaning over the railing, called to the little girl. She put K'tonton back into the pail which was now empty, and ran up the steps to her mother.

K'tonton sat among the toys on a shelf in Ilsa's room while she talked to him.

"I'm your big sister, Ilsa," she said. "You must do everything I tell you, Hansel."

"I'm not Hansel," K'tonton said. "I'm K'tonton."

"No!" Ilsa said firmly. "You're my little brother, Hansel.

Now you must eat your supper." She dipped a doll spoon into a saucer of cracker crumbs and milk.

K'tonton felt tight and unhappy inside. How could he escape from this little girl who wouldn't let him be himself, but called him Hansel? He was very hungry, but he shut his lips tight. He would not let anyone turn him into a baby.

From somewhere in the apartment came the sound of a violin. K'tonton had often heard his friend, David, practicing the violin, but it didn't sound like this. The music made K'tonton think of wind running through the grass; of water rippling; of being out in the night with one's father, looking up at the moon. It made him feel quiet inside.

"Ilsa doesn't understand," he told himself. "She's much younger than I am, even if she *is* bigger. And she saved me from being buried in the sand. It won't hurt to let her pretend I'm a baby . . . for a little while."

K'tonton opened his mouth for Ilsa's spoon. After she had given him his supper, Ilsa said, "Now you must go to sleep like a good child, Hansel." She covered him with a handkerchief and tip-toed out of the room.

The next morning K'tonton overheard Ilsa's mother speaking to Ilsa's father.

"The child is talking to an imaginary person again," her mother said. "This time she calls him her brother. Do you think you could take her with you to the rehearsal, Louis? It might distract her. You told me she is no trouble."

"I don't think anyone would mind," said Ilsa's father. "She listens so quietly. Like a little mouse!"

So Ilsa went to the orchestra rehearsal with her father,

and K'tonton went along. The doorman patted her head when they came in. A man with a big cello between his knees, waved to her.

They sat down in the front row of a big hall, rows and rows of empty seats behind them. On the stage, the musicians were tuning up their instruments.

A man with a baton in his hand went up on the stage and faced the musicians. The violinists put their hands to their bows. Everyone was waiting.

"Now you must be very quiet, Hansel." Ilsa whispered, a finger to her lips, "That's the conductor. Don't talk any more, just listen."

The conductor raised his baton. The music began. K'tonton couldn't have talked if he had tried. He was too full of the music. It was like all the sounds of the ocean together. It was like the forest with wind running through the trees, and leaves dancing and sunbeams dancing. He tried to see which sound came from which instrument. Was it the flute that was calling like a bird? Or was it a violin?

Now the man was waving his baton hard. Crash! Boom! Crash! went the cymbals and the trumpets and the drums. It was like forest trees falling down. It was like people running.

K'tonton didn't try to see where the sounds were coming from any more. He just listened. After a while, the music grew quiet again. K'tonton thought of the new village. He thought of his trees growing on the mountainside, drinking up water, sending their roots down into the cracks between the rocks . . .

106

Lost in the Big Pipes

K'TONTON was running along the sidewalk on his way to the beach when he noticed the big car. Ilsa had set him down for a bit of exercise and he had raced ahead. Now he waited near the big hotel for Ilsa to catch up with him.

The car was a low streamlined model, parked close to the curb.

"I'll be right back," the driver said to the man and woman in the rear seat. "Then we'll go on to Ashkelon." He went into the hotel, leaving the car door open.

K'tonton remembered that he had set out to see the whole land from Dan to Beersheba. Ashkelon was south on the way to Beersheba. This was his chance to get a ride. He ran to the open door, reached up his hands and hoisted himself to the car floor. As he settled down under the driver's seat, he remembered Ilsa.

What would she think when she found him gone? He was sorry about disappointing Ilsa. "But her mother will be pleased," he told himself. "She doesn't like Ilsa to talk to me. She calls me 'imaginary.'"

The driver had returned and was helping an important-looking man into the car. Then he got in himself. The door slammed shut. They were on their way.

K'tonton knew about Ashkelon from the story of Samson in the Bible, but he didn't know about the pipe factory in Ashkelon. When the car stopped at last and everybody got out, K'tonton looked around expecting to see wheat fields and foxes like the ones that Samson had caught. Instead, he found himself in a big fenced-in place with noise, machinery, and men working. Sparks flew. Hammers clanged. Huge concrete mixers whirled!

A guide, who had come out of a little house near the gate, explained that the giant concrete pipes were to carry water from the Jordan River to the Negev. K'tonton was very excited when he heard this, and listened carefully. But after awhile the man from the big hotel—K'tonton guessed he was a Very Important Person—began asking questions all about length and diameters and volume of flow, and processes, and other things that K'tonton didn't understand. So he thought he'd go over and take a look at the pipes. They were GIGANTIC!

K'tonton guessed that not even Samson, who had carried off the gates of a city, could have lifted one of those pipes. When he went inside, he felt like an ant crawling through a tunnel. The tunnel stretched on and on. K'tonton, whose feet had grown stiff during the long car ride, couldn't help running the length of it. When he came to the end of the first pipe, he ran the length of the next one and then the next. Thoughts running through his mind kept time with his feet.

"Soon water will be flowing through these pipes . . . water from the Jordan . . . to water the desert . . . to make it green. Trees will grow . . . wheat will grow . . . flowers will spring up, poppies and roses and crocuses and anemones. The Bible said this would happen."

K'tonton stopped running and recited out loud:

The wilderness and the dry land will be glad,
The desert shall rejoice and blossom.

The words bounced against the tunnel top and echoed back. K'tonton laughed in delight and tried it again. "Be glad!" he shouted.

"Glad," came the echo.

"Rejoice," K'tonton called.

"Joy!" said the echo.

BE GLAD . . . glad!

REJOICE . . . joy!

SING . . . sing!

Words and echoes bounced happily back and forth. K'tonton tried it in one tunnel, another, and still another. He flopped down at last, too tired to take another step. This had been a hard day.

But the Bible words were still on K'tonton's lips. Now he said them softly in the singing tones his father used to use. The chant faded to a murmur, quiet and sleepy like a lullaby. K'tonton's eyes closed, opened, closed again. He had sung himself to sleep.

When K'tonton awoke, he was in thick darkness. For a moment he thought that the pipes had already been laid in the ground for the water to flow through. It wasn't a pleasant thought. K'tonton wanted water to flow to the Negev, but he didn't want it to flow over *him*. Then he realized that he had fallen asleep and that this was the darkness of night.

K'tonton tried crawling through the darkness to the opening of the pipe. But even on his hands and knees, it wasn't easy. Now he found himself going uphill against the curving side. Now he was zigzagging down.

"I'll call," K'tonton decided. Maybe somebody will hear me. I don't suppose that everybody has gone away."

"Yoo-oo! Is anybody here?" he shouted. "Yoo-oo!"

"You!" It was the echo that answered.

"I know I'm here," K'tonton said impatiently, not so pleased with the echo as he had been by daylight. "Is anybody else here?" His last words rose to a shout.

A light flashed in the darkness. "Who's calling? Where are you?" came a voice.

A boy, carrying a lantern in his hand, stood in a circle of light. He moved slowly forward, holding the lantern before him.

"It's me. I'm right here," K'tonton answered, just in time to keep the boy's feet from coming down on him. The boy looked at K'tonton and stared.

110

"It's a pigmy!" he exclaimed. Then to K'tonton, "There isn't much to you, is there?"

K'tonton could tell by the boy's voice that he was laughing.

"I'm not a pigmy," K'tonton said with dignity. "My father and mother are regular-sized. I just happened to be born little. I'm Isaac Samuel ben Baruch Reuben, come up to the Land of Israel from America."

"And I'm Naḥum, come up to Israel from Iraq," said the boy. "But I'm almost a sabra," he added quickly. "I was just a baby when my family came to Israel."

K'tonton, whose curiosity *never* left him, asked, "How is it you're here so late?"

"My father is the night watchman. I bring him his supper every night," Naḥum answered.

He gave K'tonton a warm, friendly smile. "Maybe *you'd* like some supper? You're welcome to come home with me, Isaac . . ."

"You can call me K'tonton. Everybody calls me K'tonton."

So K'tonton hurried out of the big pipe and went home with Naḥum, swinging on the handle of his lantern.

The lamplight in Naḥum's kitchen flickered, sending shadows dancing on the white-washed walls. It reached into the next room where Naḥum's mother and his brothers and sisters lay asleep.

K'tonton sat cross-legged on the kitchen table, nibbling at the peppery *falafel* Naḥum had warmed up for him.

111

While he ate, he talked and talked. Usually K'tonton was not a big talker, but something seemed to have gotten into him that night. Maybe it was the hurt feeling at being laughed at for his littleness. Maybe he was trying to prove that Nahum had been mistaken when he had said, "There isn't much to you."

Not only did K'tonton tell Nahum how he had come to be in the pipe, but he told him about all the other places he had been to. He described all the adventures he had had, the important people he had met, and what a learned man his father was.

The *falafel* had become quite cold by now, but K'tonton was so intent on what he was saying that he hardly noticed what he was eating—until a peppery bit went down the wrong way. That set him coughing and choking, and he stopped talking.

But now Nahum began. Perhaps Nahum wanted K'tonton to know that he, too, had a scholar in his family. The scholar was his big brother. He was so smart in school, Nahum said, he had been given a scholarship to go to a higher school. You call it Technion. When he graduated, he would be an engineer. An engineer, Nahum explained, is a very important person, more important even than a foreman. When you are an engineer, you can tell the boss how to make his pipes strong, how to build a bridge or a new road, or make machinery, or even find water.

Once he had visited the Technion. There were many buildings, very big and beautiful. One had real machinery, the same as in a factory. His brother had taken him into a room that had rows of sinks and burners, and had let him look into a microscope.

Microscope! That was a new word for K'tonton. He asked Naḥum what a microscope was.

"It's to magnify something," Naḥum explained.

But "magnify" was also a new word to K'tonton, so Naḥum had to do more explaining.

"In the microscope," he said, "there is a place for a little glass shelf. You put a very, very small thing on the glass. Then you look through a tube with a lens, and the little thing gets big."

K'tonton grew so excited, he almost slid off the table. In Haifa, at the top of Mount Carmel, there was a school with a machine that made *little things big*. It seemed too wonderful to believe. But wonderful things had happened before on Mount Carmel. Wasn't it on Mount Carmel that Elijah the prophet had worked his wonders?

You know, of course, that a microscope doesn't really *make* small things big. It only makes them *seem* big. But K'tonton didn't know this. A plan was forming in his mind. In the morning he would set out for Haifa. He would find the wonderful machine, sit down on the glass shelf and grow big. Then nobody would ever again say, "There's not much to you, is there?"

"V. 'hat did you say the name of the school was?" asked K'tonton.

"Technion," said Naḥum.

"And the machine?—Mi . . . mi . . ."

"Microscope," said Naḥum.

114

K'tonton took his tiny pencil and a bit of paper out of his pocket and wrote down the important words.

Haifa
Technion
Microscope

Before the sun rose next morning, K'tonton was on his way. On the kitchen table lay a note for Naḥum:

Dear Naḥum,
Thank you for saving me from the pipes and for the falafel. *And thank you for telling me about the microscope. I am going to Technion to get big. When I come back, you won't have to carry me on your lantern. I will walk beside you.*

Shalom uvrakhah!
K'tonton

Size Isn't Everything

FROM Ashkelon, K'tonton had meant to head south to Beersheba. Now he changed his plans and turned north again. He made the first part of the journey by bus, holding on to a shoelace of an old man who was carrying a live chicken by its legs. Feathers from the chicken kept floating down, brushing against K'tonton's nose and mouth. The bus was crowded, the air close.

When they got out in Tel Aviv, K'tonton decided to hitch his next ride *outside* of a car—which he did, squeezed behind a license plate.

Through the Sharon valley, past groves of orange trees, the car sped. K'tonton sniffed happily, glad that there was no glass between him and the sweet smell of the orange blossoms.

Riding on the outside of the car grew less pleasant after

they had passed the groves. The sun beat down. K'tonton's seat felt like a hot stove.

"I'm melting," K'tonton told himself. "If we don't stop soon, I'll be nothing but a glob of fat."

But now the car swerved around a bend. Suddenly the air grew fresh and cool. K'tonton saw at once what had caused the change. It was the eucalyptus trees that bordered the road, two rows on each side.

'I'll drop pennies in my blue-and-white box every day, not just before *Shabbat*," K'tonton decided. "Then the Jewish National Fund can plant trees on every road."

The car reached Haifa at last. K'tonton slid to the ground and looked down. Below were the blue waters of the harbor. Big ships lay at anchor. He looked up. The city had climbed a mountain. White houses, sparkling in the sun, peeked from between cool pine trees and bright gardens.

K'tonton's heart beat fast. This was Mount Carmel. At the top was the school he had come so far to find—the school with the wonderful machine, Microscope, that would make him big.

A student was standing at the curbstone, trying to hitch a ride up the Carmel. He had set down a package he was carrying. K'tonton slipped into the wrappings—where the paper folded over—just as a small compact car came to a stop. The student picked up the package and hopped in, not knowing that he was taking with him another hitch hiker, a tiny thumb-sized one.

So it was that K'tonton arrived at the Technion, and was left in a package on a desk in a sunny office.

117

A sign on the desk read:

A. Carl

K'tonton heard a door shut with a bang, then open again. He waited for a moment. Then he slipped out of the wrappings of the package and looked up—into a man's startled eyes. The startled look quickly changed to a smile of welcome.

"*Shalom*, K'tonton," said the man. "I expected you'd get to Israel some day."

Now it was K'tonton who looked surprised. This was the second time a stranger had recognized him since he had arrived in Israel.

"I'm Mr. Carl," the man went on. "You don't know me, but I remember you. We've met before in America."

He put out his hand and K'tonton shook it. Not the whole hand! The little finger was as much as K'tonton could manage.

"Is there something I can do for you, K'tonton?" Mr. Carl asked.

"If you please, could you take me to the machine that makes little things big?" K'tonton glanced at the slip of paper in his jacket. "You call it . . . Mic . . . Microscope. It *is* here, isn't it?"

"We have many microscopes here," said Mr. Carl. "What do you want a microscope for?"

"So I can get big," K'tonton answered, surprised that Mr. Carl should ask. Naḥum . . . he's a friend I met in the pipe factory—his brother goes to school here—Naḥum said if you put something very small on the glass shelf and look through a kind of tube, the small thing gets big. Please, sir," K'tonton said eagerly, "will you put *me* on the glass so I can grow big."

Mr. Carl picked up K'tonton in his hand. "K'tonton," he said gently, "I'm afraid you didn't quite understand your friend, Nahum. The little thing on the slide—slide is what we call the glass shelf—the little thing doesn't really get big. It just *looks* big. When you take it off the glass, it's as little as before. Besides, you're too big to fit on the glass. The things Nahum's brother looked at were so tiny you couldn't even *see* them without the microscope."

Disappointment choked K'tonton's throat, looked out of his eyes.

"Why do you want to be big?" Mr. Carl asked. "I like you as you are."

K'tonton blinked back a tear. "Because if *you're* big, you can do big things."

"I know some *little* things that can do big things," said Mr. Carl. "Come! Let me introduce you to them."

So K'tonton began what Mr. Carl called his "special course at the Technion."

"Lesson I," said Mr. Carl, as he carried K'tonton into a big room he called a biology lab. It was after school hours, and the students had all left.

"There's the microscope you're so interested in," Mr. Carl said, and he set K'tonton down on a table near something with a stand, a long tube, and a little glass shelf. K'tonton saw at once that he could not have fitted on that glass. It was comforting to know that he was too *big* for something, but not comforting enough to make up for his dreadful disappointment. He had so wanted to be big. He had been so sure he was going to be big.

"Look at this slide, K'tonton." Mr. Carl pointed to the oblong glass.

K'tonton looked. All he saw was a drop of water.

"Now look at it through the microscope."

Mr. Carl held K'tonton up to the lens and K'tonton pressed an eye against it. The drop of water turned into a pond with tiny wriggling creatures swimming around.

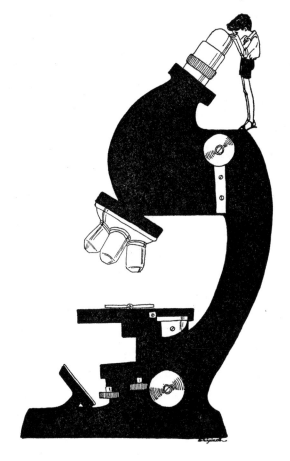

"Do you know what these tiny creatures can do?" said Mr. Carl. "They can make a strong man sick. And these" . . . he pointed to another slide . . . "can make a sick man well."

K'tonton hardly heard him. He was too busy being sorry for himself because the microscope couldn't help *him*.

"Maybe Lesson 2 will go better," said Mr. Carl. "We'll try the Mining Engineering Department."

He carried K'tonton into another building. Specimens of rocks and metals of every kind and color were arranged on shelves.

"Which do you think is the most precious?" Mr. Carl asked.

K'tonton didn't answer.

"That one is." Mr. Carl pointed to the smallest stone of all. "It's a diamond."

"I know," said K'tonton. "You put diamonds in rings."

"And in watches to make them go, and in machines to drill and to grind. These tiny stones can cut the hardest rock."

K'tonton was no longer listening.

"Well, there's still Lesson 3," said Mr. Carl hopefully.

This time he carried K'tonton across the campus to a lecture hall in a fine new building.

K'tonton saw rows and rows of seats. Up front was a desk with a blackboard behind it. A chalk diagram of big circles and little circles and pointing lines was drawn on the blackboard.

"That's a drawing of something we call an atom," Mr.

Carl said, "but a million, billion times bigger than it really is. You know the size of a toy balloon, K'tonton?"

K'tonton nodded.

"Well, you could put a hundred million, billion atoms in one toy balloon. That's how tiny they are. And do you know what those tiny atoms will do for us when our students learn how to put them to work? They'll make electricity for our homes and our factories. They'll run our ships. They'll help doctors make people well. They'll even move mountains, if we want them to!"

This time K'tonton's eyes were sparkling with excitement.

"That's what atoms can do," Mr. Carl went on. "And they're so tiny you can't see them even with a microscope —not even with an electronic microscope. That's the most powerful kind of all. Do you still think little things can't do big important work?"

It would have been better if Mr. Carl had not mentioned the microscope. The word set K'tonton thinking again about his big mistake. The sparkle left his eyes.

Mr. Carl looked discouraged for a moment. Then a gleam came into his eyes. Back across the campus he went, K'tonton tucked into his pocket. Students nodded to him as he passed. A tall professor stopped to ask if he could spare a few minutes. There was something he wanted to discuss. Mr. Carl asked him if it could wait until the next day. He had an important visitor from America.

Back in his office, Mr. Carl took a map out of a drawer and spread it wide on his desk. It was a map of the world.

"K'tonton," Mr. Carl said, setting him down on the map. "Can you find America for me?"

K'tonton found it.

"Europe? Asia? Africa?"

K'tonton found them all.

"Now the Mediterranean Sea," said Mr. Carl.

K'tonton found the Mediterranean Sea, and many countries on the shores of the sea: Italy shaped like a boot, Greece, Turkey, Egypt.

"Where is Israel?" Mr. Carl asked.

Israel was harder to find. It was so tiny. When K'tonton tried to point to it, his finger touched its neighbors Lebanon, Syria, and Jordan.

"H'm," said Mr. Carl. "Israel can't be very important. It's just a speck on the map."

"But, Mr. Carl, Israel is *very* important!" K'tonton sprang to Israel's defense. "It's the land God promised to Abraham. The whole Bible came from Israel. And now . . ."

A twinkle in Mr. Carl's eyes made K'tonton stop in the middle of his sentence. Now he knew what Mr. Carl had been trying to teach him.

"I guess size isn't everything," he admitted. And he grinned up at Mr. Carl.

The disappointment in K'tonton's heart had melted away. He and the State of Israel were both *k'tontons*.

From K'tonton's letter to his Parents:

> . . . *So now I am in the Technion, but I will*

not be here long, because I am going to Beersheba with Naḥum's brother. Mr. Carl found him for me. I told him I was going to Beersheba where Abraham-our-Father used to live. He said, "I am going down that way myself to work on a reactor. We can go together."

Do you remember that I wrote you about Meirke, Shimshon's nephew that I met on Pesaḥ? He lives in Beersheba. He invited me to visit him, so maybe I will stay with him.

K'tonton Goes Up in a Rocket

WHAT you are going to hear now is different from any of K'tonton's other adventures. We cannot even be certain it actually happened. When we asked K'tonton, he didn't say "yes" and he didn't say "no." He shut his lips tight. It is called "classified information."

The one who told us about this—we shall call him The Informant—heard it from a friend X who knew a young man Y who was assistant to the great scientist Z. Perhaps we had better not call the scientist Z. So many letters may be confusing. We will just call him the Great Scientist.

It happened in the Negev, not far from Beersheba. Do you remember when Israel sent a small rocket into space? There was a rumor at the time that the rocket carried a capsule, containing a mouse. *It wasn't a mouse. It was K'tonton!*

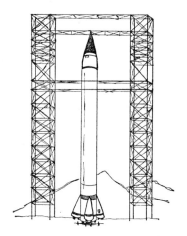

According to the Informant, the Great Scientist and his assistant were preparing the mouse for its flight, when the assistant began complaining.

"Why," he asked, "can't Israel send a man into space? We have the know-how."

The Great Scientist laughed. "In this capsule?" he asked, pointing to the little capsule into which he was fitting the mouse. "Be glad that we have a rocket big enough to send a mouse into space. It will bring back valuable information."

At that moment they heard a small voice say, "But you *could* send a person. You could send me."

The voice came from a tiny boy about the size of a thumb.

The Informant said that the Great Scientist didn't seem especially astonished. Great scientists have learned that there are many things in the world that they don't know about. When they see something new, they don't gape. They just take a notebook and a pencil and describe it. This is what the Scientist did. He wrote:

About four inches tall . . .
Looks entirely human . . .
Quite intelligent . . .
Is saying, "I'd be better than a mouse. I'm no big-
ger than one and I can talk. When I come back,
I could tell you what I had seen."

The Informant said that after this K'tonton told the Great Scientist all the things he had already ridden on: a chopping knife, a cat's tail, a yellow bird, a whizzing arrow, EL AL, a lizard. He was sure, he said, that he could ride in a rocket.

The Great Scientist tried to explain to K'tonton, in very simple, unscientific language, that the matter wasn't so easy.

"There are a lot of tests you'll have to take," he said, "health tests, whirling tests, heat and cold tests, moving faster-and-faster tests, being locked-in-by-yourself tests."

"If the mouse passed, I can pass," K'tonton said. And he *did*.

Some of the tests left K'tonton pretty shaken up, but he didn't mind. It was so exciting to be learning about things he had never known before, like gravity and weightlessness. Gravity, the assistant explained to him, is what keeps you on the ground and pulls you back if you go up in the air.

One day the Scientist showed K'tonton a picture of two

mice in a small chamber, like the capsule he was to go up in.
The mice weren't running across the floor or hiding. They
were *floating in the air.*

"That's because there is no gravity in outer space," the
Scientist explained. "If there isn't any gravity to hold you
down, you rise into the air. We call this 'weightlessness.'
When *you* go up, we can tie you down, so that you won't
float around like the mice."

K'tonton said, if they didn't mind, he'd rather not be
tied down. He wanted to see how it felt to float like a
feather. They could just pad the sides of the chamber, so
he wouldn't bump his head.

"Good!" the Scientist said. "You can also report how it
feels to eat when you are weightless. We'll give you a little
sandwich to take along."

He added that K'tonton wouldn't be up long enough to
really need food. He wasn't going into orbit. The sandwich
was purely for experimental purposes.

"What kind of sandwich would you like?" the assistant
asked K'tonton.

"*Gevinah bevakasha* cheese, please," K'tonton answered.
He liked the Israel cheese that was made of sheep's milk.

There was one special problem for the Scientist to solve.
Where could he get a space suit small enough for K'tonton? It is often harder to make tiny things than regular-
sized ones, and a space suit needs all kinds of equipment—
gadgets to keep the heat out and to bring oxygen in, air-
tight zippers, special lenses to look through, earphones to
listen with. They finally found a most exact and expert

instrument maker, a graduate of a school in Jerusalem. Not only did he make a space suit exactly K'tonton's size, but all the instruments to go with it, including the tiniest of radio sets for receiving messages and sending them.

I wish that I could tell you how K'tonton finally blasted off, what thoughts went through his mind as he entered outer space, where he came down, what he said on his return. But the Informant wasn't able to give us any information about these matters. He reported only one detail. He said that K'tonton was very much elated when he came down, until the Scientist asked him how it felt to be weightless.

"Fine," K'tonton answered, but there was a troubled look in his eyes.

"I didn't do the experiment," he said.

"What experiment?" the Scientist asked, puzzled.

"The eating one," K'tonton said, "to find out how you feel if you eat when you are weightless."

He explained that he had just recited the blessing over food, when his sandwich floated away. Of course he went after it. But this was as hard as trying to catch a runaway balloon—harder because he and the sandwich were *both* floating. Not only that. The top of the sandwich went off in one direction, the bottom in another. By the time he had caught them both, the capsule had been ejected and was floating down to earth.

"Do you have the sandwich?" the Scientist asked.

"Yes," K'tonton answered. "I wasn't weightless any more, so there wasn't any use eating it."

129

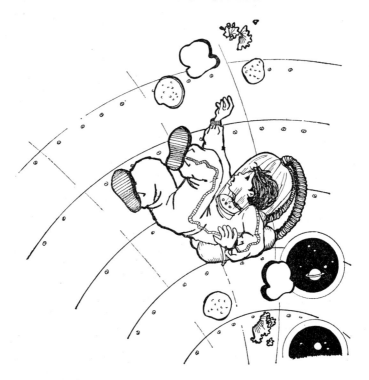

"Eat it now," the Scientist said. "You must be famished after your big adventure."

Then he told K'tonton not to worry about the experiment. "You've done a fine job," he said. "A hundred mice couldn't have given us the information that you have."

Later he told the assistant that he was greatly pleased with the results. He said that K'tonton had shown remarkable keenness of observation and real intelligence, that the findings would help them greatly in their research.

There was one more detail that the Informant reported.

130

It was something he overheard the Great Scientist say to K'tonton as they were parting.

"K'tonton," he said, "if it were up to me, I'd see that you received an honorary degree from the Hebrew University."

We must remind you again that it wasn't K'tonton who told us about this adventure. We have no proof that it happened; no proof that it *didn't* happen! You will have to decide for yourself.

To Beersheba and the Dead Sea

IT was the Technion student who brought K'tonton to Meirke's house in Beersheba. Meirke, you remember, was Shimshon's little nephew who almost didn't ask the *Mah Nishtanah* at the *seder*. He had come up to Jerusalem for Passover, but his home was in Beersheba.

K'tonton knew that Meirke's parents taught school in the old part of the city, so it wasn't hard to find them. They lived in a small white house with a walled-in garden that smelled like perfume from the jasmine.

"K'tonton must pay us a long visit," Meirke's mother said. "We have plenty of room. Not that he'll need much room."

"We'll take you to see all the sights, K'tonton," said Meirke. "Won't we, Father?"

"Will you take me to see the tamerisk tree that Abraham planted?" K'tonton asked.

132

Meirke's father explained that Abraham's tree was no longer there. "But we'll show you the new trees the school children have planted," he said. "Maybe they're descended from Abraham's tree."

Meirke and his father were proud of all the new trees in the park and along the wide streets. They were proud to point out the pottery factory and the hospital, and the new houses going up, and the new schools and the new hotel. Beersheba made K'tonton think of the Wild West, but he knew it was in the South, and there weren't any cowboys or Indians riding into town, only *kibbutzniks* in trucks and friendly Arabs.

The next day Meirke's mother took K'tonton to school with her.

"Children," she said to her class, "we have a visitor," and she pointed to K'tonton standing on her desk. "He will tell you his name and where he comes from. If you like, you may tell him *your* names, and where *you* come from."

A dark-eyed boy in the last row raised his hand excitedly and began jumping up and down. But the teacher paid no attention to him.

"I'm K'tonton and I come from America," K'tonton said.

The first boy in the first row said, "I'm Moshe and I come from Algiers."

The blue-eyed boy behind him said, "I'm Shlomo from Roumania."

"I'm Mazel from Aden," said the thin little girl with a shawl around her head.

"I'm Sarika from Libya," said the dark-skinned one.

"I'm Esther from Iran."

K'tonton was surprised to hear how many countries the pupils had come from. He counted *seventeen!*

The boy in the back seat, who had been jumping up and down and waving his hand all this time, got his turn at last.

"I'm Shalom from Morocco, don't you remember me, size-of-a-thumb one?" he said, all in one breath.

It was Shalom whom K'tonton had met at the President's reception in Jerusalem. Shalom told the class how K'tonton danced before the President and how he fell into his mother's lunch bag. The children thought this very funny. Then K'tonton told them how he went up Mount Zion on Shalom's foot.

After class, Shalom asked Meirke's mother if he could take K'tonton home with him. She said, "If he'd like to go, but be sure to bring him back."

On the way K'tonton told Shalom how he had happened to lose him on Mount Zion.

"I looked for you everywhere," Shalom said. "I even asked my sister Bracha to help me. Do you know what she said, when I told her about you? She said 'You're making up a story.' Wait until she sees you!"

They didn't have to wait long. When they turned into the main street, Bracha was standing on the corner, carrying a big tray of candies in her arms. She had very white teeth and laughing eyes like Shalom's. Big as her eyes were, they grew even bigger when Shalom held out his hand with

K'tonton on it. She was too confused to think of anything to say. She just broke off a sliver of candy and handed it to K'tonton.

"*Todah!* Thank you!" he said, nibbling at the candy. "It's very good."

"Our mother made it," said Bracha.

"Are you selling it?" K'tonton asked.

"I'm supposed to," said Bracha. "But there haven't been many buyers."

"Maybe I can help you," K'tonton offered. He had been growing less timid since his arrival in Israel. Without waiting for an answer, he hopped on the tray and began calling out:

Candies!
Delicious candies!
Home made!
Come and buy!

Passersby took him to be a mechanical toy. A crowd gathered. In no time the candies were all sold.

Bracha looked at K'tonton gratefully.

"Now I can get home early to my father," she said. "He'll be going back to work tomorrow. He only comes home once in two weeks.

"He works in the potash plant down near the Dead Sea," Shalom explained. "It's very hot down there."

"It's the lowest place in the world," said Bracha.

K'tonton knew that the Dead Sea was where the wicked cities of Sodom and Gomorrah used to be. It was where Lot's wife looked back and turned into a pillar of salt. He asked Shalom if the pillar of salt was still there.

"Of course it is," said Shalom. "I've seen it many times. Sometimes my father lets me go down on the bus with him and the driver brings me back. We could go down tomorrow, if you want to."

That's how K'tonton and Shalom happened to be in the Sodom bus next morning, squeezed in among the workmen. The bus wound down the smooth new road, through rolling bare hills. Sometimes K'tonton saw patches of green shrubs with sheep and goats grazing, or a camel, or low black tents. A woman, covered all over with a black robe, carried a white lamb in her arms. Another held a jar on her head.

"They're Bedouin, Arab shepherds," Shalom said.

"When the growth dries up in one place, they move to another."

"Like Abraham in the Bible," K'tonton thought.

136

Now the road plunged down and down. All around them were strange bare mountains that looked as if they were made of chalk-gray and white and brown chalk with swirling lines, and pieces sliced off.

The bus stopped near the potash plant.

"Don't try to take a swim," Shalom's father said, as he got off with the other workmen. "Stay right on the bus with the driver."

The bus went on. When it stopped again, the Dead Sea lay before them, blue and shining.

"Why did your father tell you not to go in the water?" K'tonton asked. It was very hot, and he would have enjoyed a swim. "Was he afraid that you would drown?"

"No," Shalom said. "He didn't want me to miss the ride back. You couldn't sink in the Dead Sea if you wanted to. The salt would hold you up."

"I guess it's the brimstone that rained down from heaven," K'tonton said.

They were standing together near the bus door—Shalom on the lower step, K'tonton on the railing.

"There's Lot's wife that you wanted to see," said Shalom, pointing.

"Where?" K'tonton looked puzzled. He didn't see anything that looked like a pillar.

"Up there! Over the salt mine," Shalom said. "That white peak!"

K'tonton looked at the peak for a long time. At first, it didn't seem like anything but a thin, jagged peak; but after awhile he could see that it was a woman turning her head to look back—a woman covered all over with hard salt.

When K'tonton looked down again, Shalom was gone. He had only run over to a pumping station nearby to talk to a friend, but K'tonton didn't know this.

A party of tourists was getting into a car. K'tonton heard the guide say they were going to Ein Gedi. Ein Gedi was in the Bible. It was one of the places where David fled when King Saul had tried to take his life. K'tonton wished that he could go along.

A woman, with a sweater on her arm, was hurrying toward the car. The sweater brushed against K'tonton as she passed. He grabbed hold of it and held on.

When the car started, K'tonton was inside.

A Ride on a Wild Goat

THE car wound through bare, stony mountains, between towering walls of rock and jumbled boulders. It climbed a hill, rounded a bend. Someone pointed. A green patch stood out against a bare mountain side.

"Ein Gedi," the driver said. "We'll go on to the springs and stop at the *kibbutz* on the way back."

They drove past green fields, orchards, a cluster of little houses, vineyards. The chug of a tractor came from a field. Again the car climbed. Then it stopped at the foot of a cliff. K'tonton looked up. A ribbon of water gushed out of a rock and leaped down the cliff into a pool. Reeds and wild flowers grew around it. Above the waterfall, other springs bubbled up.

Everybody left the car. K'tonton didn't climb up to the pool with the tourists. He stood by himself on a rock, listening to the bubbling and gurgling of the water. Now he knew why the place was called Ein Gedi. *Ein* means "spring of water." But why, he wondered, was it called Ein *GEDI*, the spring of the little goat.

The next minute he knew. Down a narrow rocky ledge, came a wild goat. Not a baby one! This goat had long horns curving over its back. It stopped directly below the rock on which K'tonton was standing, and began nibbling on a green shrub. One of its horns was so close, K'tonton touched it with his finger.

A wild thought came into K'tonton's head. "If I got on that horn, the goat would carry me high into the cliffs. Maybe I'd find David's cave up there. The Bible says King Saul pursued David to 'the rocks of the wild goats.'"

K'tonton was already sliding down the rock. He had mounted the horn, one leg on each side, hands holding tight, when the goat lifted its head and was off. Up, up into the cliffs the goat climbed on sure feet, following the narrow ledges, leaping across ravines, higher and higher. K'tonton grew dizzy looking down.

Suddenly the goat stopped and lowered its head. Down from its horn, over the ledge went K'tonton. Luckily he didn't fall far. A little way below, on a shelf of rock, a bird had built its nest—a big untidy nest of piled-up sticks. Into the nest K'tonton tumbled. The nest was an old one with no birds or eggs inside. This was fortunate for K'tonton, because it was a vulture's nest and a vulture is as big and fierce as an eagle.

Beside the nest was a large opening in the cliff. K'tonton

clambered over the side of the nest, made his way carefully along the ledge and looked in. *It was the mouth of a cave.* K'tonton's heart thumped as he stepped inside. The light was too dim for him to be sure, but it seemed to him that there was another opening at the far end. Did the opening lead to an inner cave deep in the mountains? *Could this be the cave where David spared King Saul's life?* The Bible said that Saul and his captain entered the cave and lay down to sleep, not knowing that David and his men were in the *inner* part.

K'tonton could see it clearly in his mind: Saul lying asleep in the front part of the cave, right here where he was now standing. David watching from the opening in the rear. Now David and his nephew came stealing quietly toward Saul.

"God has put your enemy into your power," the nephew is saying. "Let me run my spear through him."

But David answers, "God forbid! He is our annointed King. I will but cut off the hem of his robe. Later, when he sees it in my hand, it will be proof to him that I mean him no harm."

K'tonton was glad that David had spared Saul's life. It made him feel solemn to be in a place where such important things had happened.

"I'll explore the cave all the way back," he decided. "Maybe David's men left something behind."

The air in the cave was musty and smelled of bird droppings. The deeper K'tonton went, the darker it grew. He could just about see his hands in front of him. It was scary to be walking in the darkness. Something shadowy flew overhead. K'tonton jumped, then scolded himself.

"It's probably just a bat," he said. "Bats live in caves. I never heard of a bat hurting people."

But he didn't feel quite easy. He was so small, the bat might not know he was a person.

"I'd better turn back," he decided.

But something didn't let K'tonton turn back. It was the feeling that just ahead, maybe a few steps away, something exciting might be waiting for him—an ancient spear or a water jug.

"I'll take one more look," he decided.

He peered around him in the darkness. He strained his eyes to see ahead. He looked down. Something was shining on the floor—something white and very small. He bent quickly and picked it up. It was a tiny scrap of parchment. K'tonton couldn't see whether there was writing on it. Probably not! It was such a little piece. He wished he had found a scroll of parchment, instead of just a scrap. Not even a spear would be as exciting as a scroll—even a tiny scroll, the kind rolled up in a *Mezuzah*. A question came into K'tonton's mind. What did people who lived in caves do about a *Mezuzah?* You were supposed to put one on the doorpost of your house. But a cave didn't have a doorpost. Did they put one up near the mouth of the cave? Maybe what he had found was a tiny piece of *Mezuzah* scroll, that had fallen out of its case!

K'tonton stuck his find into his pocket and made his way back to examine it in the light. But he never got the chance. When he reached the opening of the cave, he heard a loud, rushing noise. A wind was blowing, a hot wind, full of swirling sand. The sand stung K'tonton's cheeks. He put his hands over them, and tried to get back into the cave. It was too late. The wind swooped down, lifted him off his feet, and whirled him away—over mountains, over hills. K'tonton shut his eyes to keep out the sand.

That was the last that he remembered.

When K'tonton opened his eyes again, the wind had gone. He was lying under a tamerisk tree near a low black tent. A young boy, very brown from the sun, was pouring water over his hands and feet.

For a minute K'tonton thought that he had been whirled back into the Bible days.

"Are you Isaac?" he asked the boy.

The boy shook his head. "Selim!" he said, pointing to himself.

K'tonton realized that he was in one of the Bedouin camps he had seen from the bus window that morning.

Now Selim brought K'tonton a bit of flat bread and goat cheese to eat. K'tonton, who was very thirsty, opened his knapsack and held up his tiny cup. Selim smiled and filled it with goat's milk.

"He couldn't be kinder to a stranger if he really were Abraham's son," K'tonton thought. Then he remembered that Abraham was the father of the Arab people, just as he was the father of the Jewish people.

Soon K'tonton and Selim were talking together. Selim knew a few Hebrew words, and K'tonton understood a few Arabic words that sounded like Hebrew. But mostly they talked with motions.

Selim raised his hand toward the sky, making a whooshing sound like wind, then moved his finger quickly downward to show that K'tonton had been dropped down by the wind.

"Here?" K'tonton asked, pointing to the ground under the tree.

Selim shook his head, and ran over to a loom that rested on flat stones in front of the tent. Again he made the whooshing sound, this time pointing to the half-woven cloth on the loom. Then he made a sweeping motion of his hands, as if he were scooping up K'tonton from the cloth, and ran back to the tree.

Now K'tonton knew why there were no bruises on his body. He hadn't landed on the ground. He had come down on the soft and bouncy loom.

They were still speaking when Selim's mother came out of the tent, sat down on the ground before the loom, and began to weave. She was making a new goat's hair covering for their tent. K'tonton couldn't see her face. It was mostly covered by a black shawl. But he watched her hands. In and out, in and out, went the shuttle in her quick fingers.

A chicken hopped on the loom and Selim chased it off. Then he picked K'tonton up and carried him outside the camp where the flocks were grazing; black goats with long shaggy hair and drooping ears, sheep, and snowy lambs.

K'tonton laughed at a tiny kid, waving its tail fast like a fan. He threw back his head to get a look at a tall, long-legged camel. The camel didn't have very good manners. It stuck its nose into the air and humpfed most unpleasantly. But K'tonton soon forgave it, because the next morning this very camel carried him back to Beersheba.

It was a Thursday. K'tonton had had a good night's sleep, lying in the tent on a sheepskin beside Selim. Now he rode high up on the camel's back, tucked into the cord around Selim's headscarf. The camel grunted and grunted. But K'tonton didn't mind. He felt as if he had gotten into a Bible story.

The market outside Beersheba was crowded with donkeys and camels, with Bedouin and tourists, and people selling things. A girl, carrying a tray of candies, moved among the tourists.

"Bracha!" K'tonton called.

The next minute he was standing once more on Bracha's tray.

"*Maa is-salaam, Salem ee-dek!*" K'tonton said, trying to say "good-bye" and "thank you" to Selim in his own language.

"*Shalom!*" Selim answered in Hebrew. He smiled a broad smile, pleased with himself for having brought K'tonton back to his friends.

An Important Discovery

IT was Friday night. Meirke's mother had kindled her Sabbath candles. All the family were gathered around the table—the baby in his highchair, K'tonton on a special stool set up for him on the tray. He was clean and fresh. Meirke's mother had given him a bowl of warm water to bathe in, and had washed out his underclothes and white shirt.

"Tell us again what happened to you, K'tonton," Meirke begged. "Tell us right from the beginning."

Once more K'tonton told them about his ride to the Dead Sea with Shalom; about the wild goat he had met in Ein Gedi, how it had carried him on its horns, high up into the cliffs.

When he came to the part about the cave, Meirke's father asked, "Did you notice any jars in the cave, K'tonton? Sometimes, old rolls of parchment are found in those caves, hidden in clay jars."

Suddenly K'tonton remembered the scrap of parchment he had picked up from the cave floor. So much had happened since then, he had completely forgotten it. He stuck his hand into his pocket. It was still there.

"I didn't see any jars," K'tonton said. "I just found this." He held out his hand with the bit of parchment in it. Meirke's father looked very interested. "Fetch me my magnifying glass, Meirke," he said. "Better bring along the tweezers we use for butterflies."

Meirke brought them quickly.

Carefully, his father picked up the bit of parchment with the tweezers and examined it under the magnifying glass. There *was* writing on it—a tiny *shin*. *Shin* is the first letter in the *Shema*.

Everyone crowded around and looked at the little letter in wonder.

Meirke's father was the first to speak. "This may be part of a scroll from a *mezuzah* or a pair of *tefillin*," he said. K'tonton had forgotten that *tefillin*, the little leather cases worn in prayer, also contained tiny scrolls. "It should be sent to the Hebrew University. Where there is one piece of parchment, there may be others."

He turned to K'tonton. "I don't know whether David was once in that cave, but I wouldn't be surprised if some of Bar Kokhba's men were there. You know about Bar Kokhba, don't you, K'tonton?"

Of course K'tonton knew about Bar Kokhba. Every year on Lag Ba'Omer his father made him a tiny wooden sword. Then they went to the woods, and he pretended he was one of Bar Kokhba's brave fighters trying to drive the Roman armies out of their land.

"What you found in the cave," Meirke's father said, "may be something left by Bar Kokhba's soldiers or their families. We know that they hid out in those caves near the Dead Sea. They had made up their minds to die rather than surrender. What do you say, K'tonton? Shall we send your find to Jerusalem?"

K'tonton nodded solemnly.

"Then right after *Shabbat,* you and I will write a letter to Shimshon in Jerusalem. We will ask him to go up to the University to tell the professors about your discovery. You will have to write down everything that happened—where you met the wild goat, which way it went, about the bird's nest in front of the cave, what you found inside."

K'tonton was almost bursting with excitement.

"Don't expect too much, K'tonton," Meirke's father warned him. "Nothing may come of this, after all. Then again, something might."

This is as much of the adventure as K'tonton told us. We know, however, that many months later, when K'tonton was no longer in Beersheba, one of the professors of the Hebrew University, together with a party of volunteers, made an expedition to the Dead Sea caves. It was a daring expedition. *They* didn't have wild goats to carry them up the steep cliffs. They had to *climb* the narrow ledges on their own feet, and swing one another across ravines on ropes.

But the search was rewarded. Deep in the caves they found old coins, arrowheads, a woman's comb, belts, olive pits, many things which showed that men and women had lived in the cave in the time of Bar Kokhba. They also brought back sections of tiny scrolls, the kind that are used in *tefillin*. But these weren't found in the cave. They were discovered in a vulture's nest. The newspaper report said that the bird had found them in a cave and had "disrespectfully used them as building material." The report also said that an "anonymous American friend" had provided the clue which led them to the caves.

Could the American friend have been K'tonton?

A letter from K'tonton to his friend David in America:
> *David habibi,*
>
> *This is how you say "Dear David" in Hebrew. I wish you were here. Last week I discovered a cave high up in the cliffs. A wild goat took me there. Meirke's father said probably some of Bar Kokhba's soldiers hid there from the Roman armies. They said "We will not surrender to the Romans. We will die free men."*
>
> *It is like the story you told me about the American Revolutionary War, when Patrick Henry said, "Give me liberty or give me death." George Washington's armies won, so now we have the United States. But Bar Kokhba did not win. His men died in the cave.*
>
> *I guess I am a little homesick, but I don't want*

to come back yet because there are many more places I must see.

If you look at a map, Israel is very small. But when you are there, it is not small.

Derishat shalom *to your father and mother and your Aunt Minnie and all my friends. That is how you say "best regards" in Hebrew. Did you tell your Aunt Minnie that I thank her for bringing me to Israel?*

Now I will say good-bye to you in Hebrew and and in Arabic. Shalom! Maa is-salaam!

Your friend,
K'tonton.

P.S. *Do you know that there is a George Washington Forest in Israel? When I see Zaydeh in the tree nursery, I will tell him about Patrick Henry. Maybe they will plant a forest for him, too.*

Welcome to a Kibbutz

S HALOM! will you give me a lift?" said a thin, high voice.

The man on the combine looked down to see where the voice was coming from. On a boulder beside the road stood a tiny boy, no bigger than a thumb. He wore a cap on his head. A tiny knapsack was strapped to his shoulders.

The driver tried not to show his astonishment. Once, before he had come to Israel, he had been a stranger in a far land, and he knew how uncomfortable it was to be stared at.

"*Shalom!* Hop on," he called down pleasantly.

Then he remembered that to tell this little fellow to hop on the combine was like telling an ordinary-sized man to hop up a mountain. He leaned over and put out a hand—a brown, firm, work-calloused hand. K'tonton hopped on and was lifted to the seat.

"My name is Elli," the man said, as he started the engine and the combine rumbled down the road. "I'm from the *kibbutz* down the valley. What's your name?"

"K'tonton," the little fellow answered.

"What brings you to our parts, K'tonton?"

"I'm on a hike to see all the places where the Bible stories happened."

"You've come to the right place," said Elli. "This is where King Saul and Jonathan fought their last battles with the Philistines." He turned and pointed into the distance where a mountain rose, stark and bare. "That's Mount Gilboa where they died. Nothing grows on the mountain to this day."

"On account of what David said when he heard the dreadful news," K'tonton said. He began reciting solemnly:

> *Ye mountains of Gilboa*
> *Let there be no rain nor dew upon you,*
> *Neither fields of choice fruits. . . .*

Then his voice rose in excitement. "Do you suppose we could take David's curse off? It happened so long ago, I don't think he would mind. Do you suppose if we went up there and dug out the stones and planted trees and tended them, God would send back the rain and dew?"

"It wouldn't surprise me," said Elli. "He has helped us take the curse off a lot of places. Our own fields, for instance. This is what they used to be like."

Elli pointed to the fields they were passing. K'tonton saw stones, dry barren sand, scraggly bushes.

"Now see what they are like," said Elli, pointing ahead.

Irrigation ditches, sparkling with water, crisscrossed the meadows. K'tonton saw fields of wheat and barley, fish ponds, waving date palms, groves of fig trees, pomegranates, olives. He saw fat cows grazing in the pasture.

"Our *Kibbutz*," said Elli. "Sde Eliyahu! How would you like to stay with us awhile?"

"I should like to very much," said K'tonton.

A young girl, carrying schoolbooks in her hand, came up as Elli and K'tonton drove in on the combine.

"K'tonton, this is my daughter, Ophra," Elli said. "Ophra, this is K'tonton. He is going to stay with us for a while. Will you see that he gets a bite to eat?"

"Who can Father be talking about?" Ophra thought, looking around and seeing no one. Then her eyes fell on the seat beside her father. There stood a boy no bigger than a thumb with a wee knapsack on his shoulders.

"*Shalom*," she said quietly. No one could have told by her voice how amazed she was to see so tiny a person. Ophra's love of birds and small creatures had taught her quiet ways.

"Her name is Ophra—fawn," K'tonton thought, "and her eyes are large and gentle like a fawn's."

Ophra was holding out her books, which were bound together with a strap.

"You can ride on my books," she said, smiling. "They'll make a good swing."

K'tonton hopped on.

It was pleasant and cool in the dining hall. The blinds were drawn, the long tables set for the next meal, 'though no one had come in.

"I suppose the little fellow can eat his food from a corner of a plate," Ophra thought, as she set him on the table. "But what can he use for a spoon? Even a teaspoon is longer than he is tall."

As if he knew what Ophra was thinking, K'tonton opened his knapsack and took out a tiny plate and cup and spoon. Ophra piled the plate with cheese and cream, then filled the thimble-sized cup with milk.

Sparrows flew overhead beneath the roof beams, chirping as K'tonton recited the Grace after Meals.

"They nest in the eaves," Ophra explained.

"There's a psalm about the birds," K'tonton said:

> *Yea, the sparrow has found a house,*
> *And the swallow a nest for herself,*
> *Where she may lay her young.*

"We have many birds here, nests too," said Ophra. "Would you like to see some?"

K'tonton hopped back on her books and they set out. A bird alighted on the faucet of an irrigation pipe, and almost turned a somersault trying to get the drip into its mouth. Long-legged herons flew overhead on their way to the fishponds. From behind a barn came a turtle dove's mournful "tur-r-r."

Ophra showed K'tonton its sprawly nest made of twigs and straw. Then she looked inside the barn and pointed upward. Swallows flitted in and out among the shadows. Plastered against a rafter, high up near the roof, was a neat nest made of mud and straw.

"I wonder if there are eggs inside," said Ophra.

"I'll find out for you," said K'tonton.

Before Ophra could stop him, he had slid down the bookstrap and was running across the barn floor. A long rope dangled from the rafter to the floor. K'tonton took hold of it, his fingers barely reached around the thick rope. Hand over hand he climbed, higher and higher and higher. Now he reached the top. Now he was running along the rafter toward the nest.

" He'll fall. Oh, he'll fall! The rafter is so narrow." Ophra shut her eyes tight, so as not to see. But the rafter didn't seem narrow to K'tonton. For him it was a broad street. He reached the nest and kneeled down, leaning over to look inside.

The next minute his voice came down to Ophra, clear and shrill above the twittering of the swallows.

"There *were* eggs, Ophra. Now there are babies. They're all bills!"

"Tsi, tsi, tsi, tsi, tsi. . . ."

The mother swallow had returned and was fluttering back and forth, chirping in distress, scolding K'tonton.

"She's frightened," K'tonton thought. "She thinks I want to hurt her babies. She loves them . . . the way my mother loves me."

Suddenly a heaviness crept into K'tonton's heart, the kind of heaviness he had felt on the day he met the colt with its mother.

K'tonton wanted to go home to his mother and father.

"But Eretz Yisrael *is* home," he told himself stoutly.

At that moment a glad thought danced into his mind. *"Maybe Father and Mother have gotten the tickets. Maybe they are coming to me."*

The heaviness was gone. K'tonton's feet twinkled as they raced across the rafters. Before the swallow had had time to stuff a bug down each baby's throat, K'tonton was running across the floor to Ophra.

"Ophra," he called, "could you let me have a piece of paper? I have to write a letter to my mother and father! It's very important."

Ophra gave him the paper, and watched as he took the bit of lead out of his pocket, sat down on the floor, and wrote:

Dear Father and Mother,

I miss you very much. Do you think you will have the tickets soon? Maybe you have them already and I did not get your letter. If you will send a letter care of Shimshon in Jerusalem, I will surely get it. I could not stay with him on account of wanting to see the whole land, but I always write him where I am.

Please come soon!

From me, your loving son,
K'tonton

P.S. Today I came to Sde Eliyahu. It is a kibbutz in the Beit She'an Valley. I do not know how long I will be here.

"Will you mail the letter for me?" K'tonton asked.

"I'll be glad to," Ophra answered. "But first we must find out where you are to stay tonight. I'll take you back to Father."

In the Children's House

ELLI was in the office, attending a special meeting, when Ophra came in. He interrupted the meeting to ask where K'tonton was to stay.

"In the children's house, of course," said Miriam, the kindergarten teacher. "Goodness knows he's little enough."

The committee had gone back to the business of the day. It had to do with the wheat crop which was very poor that year.

Avrom, the dairyman, was speaking. "First, there weren't enough winter rains," he grumbled. "Now, there isn't enough wheat. Next, there'll be a plague of mice."

"Why must you always expect trouble?" The others shouted Avrom down, but Elli, who was in charge of the harvesting, spoke up for him.

"Mice do follow a drought," he said. "We'd better
. . ."

K'tonton didn't learn what Elli thought they had better
do, because just then Miriam picked him up and marched
off to the children's house. And that's where the trouble
began, the next morning.

Mind you, the children's house was the pleasantest place
in the *kibbutz*, and the children took to K'tonton at once.
The trouble was that they took to him too much.

"He can live in our doll house," said four-year-old Noga,
with the light hair and mischief in her eyes. Without so
much as an "if you please," she picked K'tonton up and set
him down in a doll chair.

"Look!" she said. "He just fits."

"Let's see if he fits into the doll bed," said dark-eyed
Sarah.

"No! We need him for our boat." Three-year-old Asaph
grabbed K'tonton in a grimy fist and carried him out to the
pond.

The pond was a wooden wash tub filled with water. An
empty sardine tin floated on it. That was the boat.

Asaph stuck K'tonton in the boat and gave it a shove. It
sailed across the pond. Red-headed Benjy sent it back.
They laughed and laughed. It was fun to have a passenger
in their boat.

But it didn't seem fun to K'tonton. "They think I'm a
toy," he thought indignantly, sliding and bumping from
side to side. "They're worse than Ilsa. 'Put K'tonton in
the doll house.' 'Put him to bed!' 'No, put him in the
boat!' It's humiliating."

161

From the boat K'tonton could see the six-year-olds, brown and stripped to the waist, painting a tractor—a *real* tractor with *real* paint. True, the tractor was an old one that didn't work any more, but if you sat high up on the

162

seat, you could pretend it worked. K'tonton watched the painters dip their brushes into the can of red paint and swish them boldly, back and forth across the sides.

"Now that's what *I'd* like to be doing," he thought. "*Real* work. But does anyone ask me what I'd like to do? No! I'm a toy!"

Clang! Clang! Clang! The lunch bell rang. Asaph and Benjy rushed into the house, leaving K'tonton in the sardine tin. With no one to push the boat, it stayed in the middle of the pond. Round and round, round and round K'tonton rode, feeling sorrier and sorrier for himself.

"Maybe I can paddle the boat to shore with my hand," K'tonton thought.

He leaned over the side to try. But a sardine tin makes a very shallow boat. Water rushed in. The boat was sinking! K'tonton dived into the water, just as the boat went down, and swam to shore with firm, strong strokes. Water was dripping from his hair and clothes, when he reached dry ground. Inside the house, the children were reciting *hamotzi.*

K'tonton's stomach begged for lunch. "But I won't go in," he said firmly. "They'll say, 'Put him at the doll table. Look! He can eat!' I'm *not* a doll. I'm a person. *I'll leave Sde Eliyahu!*"

From the trees near the granary came the mournful notes of the turtle doves. "Turr, turr, turr!" They made K'tonton think of Ophra. He did *not* want to leave Ophra. K'tonton hesitated. Then he reminded himself sternly that he had not come to Israel to be a plaything, and went on.

163

K'tonton Saves the Crop
from an Army of Mice

K'TONTON did not know how long he had been on his way. It seemed hours and hours. He was in a forest of wheat. Water no longed dripped down his forehead, but sweat did. He sat down to shake the sand out of his shoes.

Sh-s-s-sh!

Something was stirring among the stalks, a gray furry something. K'tonton saw whiskers, a tail. A mouse! The mouse sniffed the air and looked around as if to make sure no danger was lurking. Then it squeaked. Out of the meadow came a second mouse. They pulled a stalk down with their teeth and began nibbling greedily, one head of grain, another, another.

K'tonton remembered the words he had heard at the meeting the night before. "First there weren't enough winter rains. Now there isn't enough wheat. Next there'll be a plague of mice."

The mice were already here.

"But there are only two mice," K'tonton told himself. "It's silly to worry about just two mice."

But what if the two were scouts sent ahead to spy out the land? What if a whole army of mice was behind them?

The first mouse had stopped eating, and had turned to the second.

Eek, eek, squeak! Keek, geek!

It sounded like squeaks, but K'tonton knew this was mouse language. What was the mouse saying? Was it telling the other mouse it wasn't right to sit there gorging themselves? They should be hurrying back to fetch their hungry brothers.

The second mouse nodded, its whiskers quivering. The two scurried off in the direction from which they had come.

K'tonton sprang to his feet, all his tiredness gone. An army of mice was on the way! They would invade the fields, devour the crops. He must warn Elli at once. He must hurry back.

But which way was "back"? The wheat stretched around him in all directions. K'tonton looked about anxiously. Ahead, where the grain grew thin, rose a tall plant, taller than a man, with flowers like bright blue globes.

"A lookout," said K'tonton. "I'll climb to the top and get my bearings."

But the plant was a thistle with sharp spikes.

"If I climb it, the spikes will tear my hands."

K'tonton hesitated. "But if I *don't* climb it, Sde Eliyahu will lose its wheat."

K'tonton grasped the stalk of the thistle. Up and up he climbed, trying to avoid the spikes, but not turning back when they scratched him. He reached the top at last and looked around. Beyond the grain field, he could see the pasture with cows swishing their tails; beyond the pasture, the granary and barns.

K'tonton fixed the direction in his mind: "Straight ahead, then turn left along the edge of the field." Then he climbed carefully down. At the foot of the thistle, he stopped for a minute to suck the scratched places on his arms. Then he set off on a run.

The sun was low in the sky when K'tonton reached the pasture. The cows were heading toward the barn. K'tonton envied them their long legs. One step of theirs covered more ground than twenty of his.

"If I could hitch a ride on the back of a cow, I'd be back in no time," he thought. "But how can I climb up?"

At that moment the cow nearest to him swished her tail to brush off a fly. K'tonton had his answer.

"I'll take hold of the cow's tail," he decided. "When she swishes it up, I can hop off on her back. It will be easy."

Grabbing the cow's tail *was* easy, though he had to climb on a stone and leap to get hold of it. Landing on her back was another matter. Up went the tail. Swish! K'tonton banged against the cow's flank. Before he could make his jump, the tail went down with K'tonton still on the end of it.

"Maybe I'll have better luck next time," K'tonton said, holding on fast.

Again a fly alighted on the cow. Again she swished her tail, banging K'tonton against her side. Again the tail moved down *before* K'tonton could jump.

Now K'tonton was not only scratched; he was black and blue. But the thought of the danger to Sde Eliyahu made him hold on for a third try. This time he made it. The tail went down, but K'tonton stayed up, safe on the cow's broad back.

The cow was moving faster now. She no longer stopped to browse along the way. The pasture gate was open. They passed through. Avrom was turning on the switch of the electric milker when they reached the stalls. K'tonton saw with relief that Elli was with him.

"Elli! Elli!" he cried. "It's happening—what Avrom said. The mice. . . ." He slid down the cow's side into Elli's hand.

Elli listened gravely as K'tonton poured out his story of the mouse scouts he had overheard, of the army of mice behind them.

"We'll harvest the wheat at once," said Elli. "Tomorrow may be too late. It's a lucky thing we live where it's dry enough to harvest at night. I guess you'll want to come along, K'tonton."

He picked K'tonton up and stuck him into his shirt pocket.

The combine coughed and rumbled as Elli drove it out of the shed, down the road to the fields. K'tonton watched in wonder, as the huge machine cut the standing grain and sucked it in to be threshed. The straw was tossed out, the kernels drawn into a big grain tank to be carried to the silo. All through the night the men worked. The sun did not stand still for them, but a full moon flooded the fields with light. K'tonton's head was nodding when the combine turned at last to the barns.

Morning brought the army of mice, squeaking, scurrying, crowding one another in their search for grain. All that they found were fields of stubble. The precious kernels were safe in the granary.

That night, after the meal was over, the people remained

in the dining hall, which was also the house of prayer, to give thanks for the harvest. All the children marched in, singing. Even the youngest ones were there. Elli led in the prayers. He stood facing the beautiful Torah Ark, with its carvings of pomegranates and bells. They thanked God who had sent the dew and rain and saved the crops from drought and plague. They thanked Him for blessing the work of their hands.

Then Elli turned toward the people. "There is one among us to whom we owe special thanks for the saving of our harvest," he said. And he told them the story of K'tonton and the mice.

"*Haydad! Haydad!* K'tonton! K'tonton!" The children cheered wildly.

K'tonton's heart warmed, as he made out the voices of Ophra and Noga, Asaph and Sarah and Benjy.

Elli silenced the children and went on. "Let us thank God," he said, "for giving K'tonton the wisdom to know what needed to be done and the courage to do it."

The next minute K'tonton was lifted high and set down on the reading stand. His arms and legs were bandaged because of the cuts. One cheek was bruised.

The head of the *kibbutz* came forward.

"K'tonton," he said, "you have been blessed with special gifts—tinyness of size and keenness of eye and ear so that you are able to go where we cannot go and see what we cannot see. Together with these gifts, you have a stout heart and a great love of the Torah. It is my pleasure to tell you that we have voted to make you an honorary member of our *kibbutz*."

170

"*Haydad! Haydad!* K'tonton is a member of our *kibbutz.*
Three cheers for K'tonton!"

This time the children could not be quieted. They
pushed back the chairs, joined hands, and danced a *horah*
around K'tonton.

K'tonton's hurt places ached. His heart beat wildly. But
his eyes were shining.

From K'tonton's Letter to his Father and Mother:

> . . . *So now I am a member of the* kibbutz *and
> you can stay with me. Elli says if you are a mem-
> ber, you can invite your father and mother. In a*
> kibbutz *you do not need much money. It is
> enough to help with the work.*
>
> *You will like it here, Father. It is just as the
> Psalm says:* "When you eat the labor of your
> hands, happy shall you be." *Mother will like it,
> too. There are flowers everywhere: roses and
> oleanders; also trees and much grass. When you
> come, Mother, I will pick you a pomegranate
> blossom like a scarlet bell.*
>
> *Please write quickly that you are coming.*
>
> Your loving son,
K'tonton

A Joyful Reunion

K'TONTON was high up in a palm tree, swinging on a cluster of dates, when Ophra came along, waving a paper in her hand.

"There's a letter for you, K'tonton," she called up. "From America! It was forwarded from Jerusalem."

K'tonton hurried down the tree trunk, using the scaly bark for a ladder. On the ground, he bent over the letter Ophra had spread out. In a moment he was on his feet, dancing with excitement.

"They're coming—my father and mother! By ship!

He took another look at the letter.

"They'll be here next week . . . I'll have to go to Haifa to meet them."

He turned five somersaults in a row before he could calm down.

Early on a Tuesday morning, K'tonton stood on Elli's shoulder in a big shed at the Haifa docks. Around him was a crowd of waiting people, their eyes on the door through which the ship's passengers were coming. The line seemed endless to K'tonton. He was surprised that so many people could get on one ship. Every few minutes someone in the crowd gave a cry and ran forward. Then there was hugging and kissing and laughing and crying.

There had been many times, since K'tonton arrived in Israel, when he had missed his father and mother. But he hadn't realized until now, when they were almost with him, how very much he had missed them.

"Suppose they don't come through the gate," he worried. "Suppose they couldn't get the papers they needed. Suppose they missed the boat. Suppose . . ."

Then the worries were over.

"Father! Mother!" K'tonton was waving, jumping up and down so excitedly, he almost tumbled off Elli's shoulder.

There was his father coming toward him, his eyes narrowing in the special smile that made K'tonton feel loved and warm inside. There was his mother with her "thank-God-you-are-safe" look.

K'tonton was in her hand. She was kissing him, pressing him tight against her cheek.

A dozen questions rushed to K'tonton's lips, but for once he couldn't ask a single one. His mother kept him too busy answering hers. Even while he answered, K'tonton's thoughts were joyfully running on to what lay ahead. He

173

would take his father and mother to all the places where he had been—and the places where he had not yet been: Galilee, Lake Kinneret, Safed, the Hulah, Eilat, King Solomon's mines. They would meet his friends, Shimshon and Hannah and Raphael in Jerusalem . . . Yonatan's family! Zaydeh in the tree nursery, and, of course, Yosef. He wasn't sure about Ilsa, but he was sure about the orchestra —and Naḥum and his brother, and Mr. Carl . . . and Meirke's and Shalom's families in Beersheba, and Selim. . . .

Suddenly, K'tonton remembered that he hadn't introduced his father and mother to the friend who was right with him.

"Father, Mother," he said. "This is my friend Elli from the *kibbutz*."

Elli, who had stepped back so that the family might have these first minutes to themselves, put out his hand in welcome.

"*Bo'a'khem leshalom*," he said. "May your coming be blessed with peace."

175

A P.S. for You

(we must have caught the habit from K'tonton)

P.S. 1   Israel is growing so fast, you are sure to find changes when you visit it. These are just a few of them:

> *There is less dust at the airport. Henrietta Szold's name has just been taken from the little street where Shimshon lived, and given to a beautiful new road that winds up a mountain to a new hospital at the top.*
>
> *Sde Eliyahu has a new synagogue.*
>
> *Most exciting, Mount Gilboa is no longer bare. If you stand in the Beit*

She'an Valley and look up at the mountain, you will see the beginnings of a new settlement. On the slopes are new trees, planted by boys and girls from all over the world.

P.S. 2   We wanted to tell you just when the adventures in our book happened. But K'tonton, who told us about them, isn't very exact about dates.

"K'tonton," we said, "you must be more careful. It makes a difference whether something happens in one year or the next."

"Why?" he asked.

You'd think he had forever.

S. R. W.

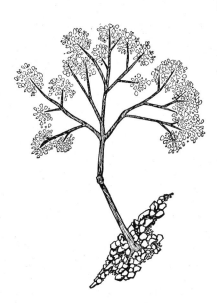